Counterfeit Dreams 5

When Dreams Aren't Enough

BLACK EDEN
PUBLICATIONS

Counterfeit *Dreams 5*

ISBN: 978-1539159834
10 9 8 7 6 5 4 3 2 1
Printed in the United States

Dedication

I would like to dedicate this book to all my readers. As most of you know, I originally intended for "Counterfeit Dreams 4: A Coke White Dream" to be the last installment of the "Dreams" series, but you guys weren't having it! It took me a while to get into the swing of things with this book because I had no idea which direction the characters wanted to go in, but it didn't take long to see each one of their paths as clear as day. This storyline really pushed me, and I hope you all can see its progression. Thank you from the bottom of my heart for all your motivation and support…I could never repay you. Now, without a further ado, I present to you "Counterfeit Dreams 5: When Dreams Aren't Enough". Enjoy!

Counterfeit

Dreams 5

When Dreams Aren't Enough

Chapter One

"Congratulations to the bride-to-be," the DJ yelled over the music that continued to play, "Whoever this nigga, he's luckier than a mothafucka."

Diamond stood up in the VIP area, raising her glass as she smiled back. *I'm the lucky one,* she thought.

It had been a year since she and Hassan had first got together, and she had never been happier. Ever since he had a conversation with Jewel about where they were in their relationship, she felt like she was finally free. She would be lying if she said that she didn't still care about Jewel anymore. He was the father of their child, and he meant the world to her, but she had to leave him in the past. Hassan was her future.

"Congratulations, bitch," Kiko sang, trying to fill Diamond's glass up to the brim with Ace of Spades.

"Naw, I'm good right now," she said shaking her head, "I'm 'bout to run to the bathroom real quick."

"Maybe you'll find Reagan's ass on the way there."

"She left?" Diamond asked setting her glass down.

"Again...," Kiko said rolling her eyes, "You hoes been acting funny all night. I wouldn't be surprised if she took her ass back to the room."

"I'll be right back," she said getting up and smoothing out her chocolate-colored and see-through mesh pants that hugged each one of her curves.

As she looked around Club Encore, she had to admit that it was smacking. She appreciated Reagan and Kiko flying her out to Vegas for her bachelorette party. She was getting married to the man of her dreams, and she had to admit that her nerves had her on edge especially after the news she had just received.

When she arrived at the bathroom, she ran right into Reagan who was making her way out. The waist-length, sandy-brown weave she adorned swung in her face as they collided.

"Hey…," she struggled to say.

"Wait for me," Diamond said as she continued to make her way inside.

Reagan did her best to avoid eye contact, but it was too late to hide the tear stains that lined her cheeks.

"That champagne's running through you, huh?" she asked, hoping to guide the conversation.

"To be honest," Diamond said through the stall, "I haven't really had any."

"Why not?" she snapped, "For $2,500 a bottle, you should be taking that shit to the head. You only get married once, right?"

Suddenly, silence filled the bathroom.

"…Diamond!"

"I'm…pregnant," she said coming out, looking down at the marble floor.

"Why you say it like that?" Reagan asked, wanting to be happy for her friend as she forced a smile upon her face. Even though they had their ups and downs over the years, she could tell that she was truly happy with Hassan and was finally ready to let Jewel go. It was refreshing to see. With their petty competition out of the way, they decided to reconcile for the sake of their kids, but Diamond continued to be there for Reagan time and time again.

"I didn't know how you would feel about it," she said finally looking up.

"It's not like it's by Jewel, right?" Reagan laughed.

"Reagan, I'm being serious," Diamond said washing her hands, staring at her through the crystal-clear mirror.

"That was almost a year ago. I gotta get over it eventually, you know?"

"You never get over losing your baby, Rea."

After Reagan and Jewel found out that they were expecting their first baby together, Reagan couldn't have been any happier. She finally felt like the universe was smiling down on her and her family, but the joy she felt was short lived. At only four months pregnant, Reagan found herself home alone, asleep in bed lying in a pool of blood. Jewel was out of town on business, so she had no choice but to get herself to the hospital. With the amount of blood she was losing, she knew she couldn't take the chance of driving herself, so she opted to call *911* instead. Luckily, Jailen and Chase were with Joe for the weekend. Within ten minutes, the paramedics were rushing her to the hospital, but as she lay in silence on the gurney, hooked up to the various monitors that sat inside, she knew that she had lost the baby. She felt empty inside. With each mile that passed, a tear slowly escaped her eyes, but she never uttered a word as she continued to listen to the sirens wail into the night.

"Listen, we're here for another day. I promise I'ma get it together," Reagan said dabbing her eyes with a Kleenex she had tucked inside her clutch, "The drank just got me in my feelings right now."

"I'll go grab Kiko, and we'll come with you," Diamond hurried to say.

"No, this is supposed to be your bachelorette party. I don't want you spending it taking care of me."

"Reagan…"

"I'm good…I swear. I'm probably just gonna go to sleep."

"You sure I can't change your mind?" Diamond hated seeing Reagan so down. She had been the epitome of strength to her despite their issues in the past. Diamond just wanted to make it better for her, but this time, she knew she couldn't.

"I'll see you in the morning. We'll do breakfast…"

"Make that brunch," Diamond said attempting to laugh.

"Brunch it is then," Reagan said smiling before she walked out of the bathroom and headed toward the elevators. Even though Hassan rented out the presidential suite for all of them, Jewel insisted that she have a room of her own. She didn't really see the need for it at the time. She loved hanging out with her girls, but tonight, she needed to be alone.

Once she got to the top floor of the Encore, she pulled her key card out of her purse and slowly slid it through the slit, revealing the barely touched room. Grabbing her phone, she decided to call Jewel. She needed his voice to soothe her, but after about four rings, there was no answer—just his voicemail.

"Hey, babe," she sighed into the phone, "I know it's late, but I just wanted to say good night. Call me when you get a chance. Love you…"

$$$$$

"Jewel…Jewel, you're phone is ringing," Khailiah said.

"Who is it?" he asked poking his head from underneath the covers as the sunlight began to peek through the ceiling-high blinds.

"Reagan…again. You gon' call her back?" she asked.

"Naw, I'll hit her back later," he said throwing the comforter back over his head hoping to drown out the morning. His head was pounding from the night before. Since the girls were in Vegas, Jewel and Sacario decided to head to Miami to let their boy live a little. At first, Jewel didn't know how he felt about Hassan and Diamond getting married, but he knew he was unable to give her what she deserved. She deserved to be loved, to be somebody's wife. It was time for him to let go.

"Listen, J," Khailiah said snatching the covers off him, "I know ya'll spent the night hoe-watching or whatever, but I think you owe me a few minutes of your time."

Knowing she was right, he rolled over exposing his broad, bare chest, giving her his undivided attention.

"Yes, Khailiah…"

"So you're on schedule to be here until tomorrow afternoon. K-2's plane lands today at 1:30 p.m., and I have a driver picking him up and bringing him to the hotel…"

"K, I trust that you got it all handled."

"Jewel, my job is to make sure you stay on track."

"And a nigga is on track, so mission accomplished. I'm here on some chill shit this weekend. I'm not too worried about work right now."

"Well, you should be. You know this money shit don't stop."

Knock. Knock. Knock. Knock.

"I got it," she said standing up, exposing her thick, caramel-colored thighs. Jewel couldn't help but to enjoy the view.

"What's up, K.K.?" Sacario asked as she opened the door.

"Trying to get this fool up. Maybe ya'll will have better luck than me," she said looking back at Jewel, "I'll let you know when K-2 gets here."

"Bye, K," he said finally getting out of bed as he put a t-shirt on.

Hassan waited until the room door closed before he spoke. "Like that?" he smiled, "Early morning, huh?"

"Don't start. It's way too early for the bullshit. Khailiah works for us. That's it…that's all."

"But it doesn't hurt that she's fine as fuck though, huh? She looks like she needs to be wifed up somewhere being waited on hand and foot."

"I guess I never noticed," Jewel said sparking up a doobie that sat in a crystal ashtray next to the bed as a smile spread across his face.

"Yeah, okay, nigga," Sacario laughed.

When Laura transferred everything to Jewel, Sacario, and Hassan, that included a few new team members—Khailiah being one of them. She was supposed to act as Executive Assistant to the three of them, but, instantly, she gravitated towards Jewel. It didn't take long before she became like his second shadow.

"Bruh, I know it's been a minute," he said sitting down, "but you can't tell me that you can't tell that she's tryna fuck."

"I mean, she's a little flirty, but she's fully aware that I'm married."

"Shit, we all are damn-near, but you know how these hoes get."

"Naw, it's not like that with K. She's just cool people, and she does her job. I don't see what the problem is."

"She's not in *our* rooms giving us no personal wake-up calls and shit," Hassan said as he broke down a swisher.

"Look, ya'll came to talk about K all goddamn day, or what?" Jewel asked beginning to get irritated.

"No, we actually came to see if you was tryna get something to eat, nigga. I'm starving."

"Hell yeah, I'm hungrier than a mothafucka. Where you tryna go?"

"Shit, this is South Beach. Take your pick."

"Alright, let me throw something on right quick," he said walking into the bathroom.

"Ay, you talk to Reagan?" Hassan asked.

"Naw, she called this morning though," Jewel said through the door, "Why, what's up?"

"Diamond called me hella late last night and was like she was going through it. They were at some club, but Reagan dipped and went back to the room by herself."

"Damn…" *I knew I shouldn't have let her go,* he thought. "I can't stay out here 'til tomorrow," he said more to himself as he came out of the bathroom half-dressed.

"You think she good?" Sacario asked, "I mean, like her mental."

"To be honest, I don't even know. Either Diamond or my dad have the kids when I'm gone. She's just been in this funk ever since we lost the baby. I've been trying, but I don't know how to pull her out of this shit."

"How you holding up, bruh?"

"I can't lie…that shit hurt like a mothafucka, but because I'm always coming or going, I guess I don't have as much time to dwell on it like she does. Ever since she franchised the gym, she's really just at home all day."

"If you gotta go check on lil' mama, go, bruh," Hassan said, "This shit ain't that important."

"Yeah, I better go," he said picking up his phone from the nightstand, "…ay, K.K., I need you."

Chapter Two

"Can you please tell me what's going on now?" Khailiah huffed as she and Jewel walked through the door to his house, "You've been quiet the whole way here."

"It's Reagan," he said, closing the door before he set his bags down in the middle of the foyer.

"What's wrong now?" she asked rolling her eyes.

"Don't do that," Jewel said turning to face her, "You know she ain't been the same since we lost the baby. It's been really hard on her, you know?"

"Yeah…I know," Khailiah said looking down at the ground, "I just hate to see you so stressed out." Slowly walking towards him, she wrapped her arms around his waist as she laid her head on his chest. Not knowing what to do, Jewel stood frozen with his hands down by his side.

"Jewel?" he heard someone say from the top of the stairs. As soon as he saw who it was, he shoved Khailiah off of him.

"Ay…Mom, what are you doing here?"

"Did you forget something, Jewel?" she asked as she sauntered down the steps never taking her eyes off of Khailiah.

"Uhhhh…I don't think so," he said appearing oblivious.

"Why am I here, Jewel?"

Fuck! he thought to himself. "My bad, Ma. I was down in Miami, and then I've been trying to get in contact with Reagan, but she's been M.I.A…."

"Jewel, Jewel, baby…none of this pertains to me. You said you were picking me up today from the airport, so I expected you to be there."

"I know...that was my fault. It won't happen again. I promise."

"Please be more aware of your commitments, son."

"How did you get here though?"

"I had a car bring me, and your father met me over here being that he's the only one of us with a spare key to this place," she said giving him the side-eye.

"My ba..."

"Khailiah, why are you here, sweetie?" Laura asked, adjusting her focus.

"Uhhhhh, I came back when Jewel did...I mean, Mr. Sanchez."

"Well, that will be all for now," she said walking into the kitchen.

Khailiah was very aware that Laura didn't play when it came to her son, so she didn't even bother to respond.

"I'll walk you out," Jewel offered, knowing better than to go against his mother's wishes, "You good?"

"Yeah, luckily, I drove over here before we left for the airport, or my ass would be striking home," she said showing off her perfect white smile.

"Now you know I wouldn't let you walk home."

"It's not you I'm worried about," she said looking back at the house, "Well, since we came back a little earlier than expected, I'll make sure your schedule is still cool for the week. You coming into the office tomorrow, right?"

"Yeah, most likely. I got some things I need to tie up."

"Okay, good, I have some paperwork I need you to sign anyway."

"Bet."

"Goodbye, Mr. Sanchez," she said before she walked over to her 2016 Mercedes CLK 350.

Jewel waited until Khailiah disappeared down the street before he made his way back inside. He had to admit that he was really digging her but not for all of the reasons everyone expected him to. Reagan still was able to give him butterflies from just a look, but he knew they hadn't been on the same page lately. If he said "black," she had to say "white," and he was honestly just tired of arguing. With Khailiah, it was effortless. She was smart, sexy, funny, but even more importantly, she got him. Jewel felt like he could let a breath escape around her, but he tried not to get too comfortable. Their relationship was strictly business.

"Jewel, come in here please," he heard Laura say from the kitchen. He already knew where the conversation was headed, but he decided to entertain her anyway.

"Yes, Mother?" he said as he walked up to the granite countertop that sat between them.

"Don't patronize me, boy," she said before taking a sip of her white Montrachet, "Why is Khailiah steadily sniffing around here like some pathetic little puppy?"

"We work together, remember?"

"Correction, Jewel, she works *for* you. There's a huge difference."

"Maybe to you…I don't operate like that, Ma. You know that."

"Yes, I do know that, and I also know that that's how you get yourself into trouble most of the time. Believe me, as soon as you start treating the help like they're your friends, they're not helpful anymore. Just look at your father and his marriage for example."

"Here you go…," he said shaking his head, "Enough about K. Let's talk about why you had to make a trip over here all of a sudden."

"K? How cute," Laura said setting her glass down on the counter, "I knew I should've went with my first instinct when your uncle hired her, but, of course, he insisted."

"Who…Steve?"

"No, Golden."

"Golden?"

"Yes, he hired her to work out here with him as his personal assistant, but you know Naidene wasn't having it, so he shipped her ass over our way."

"Why didn't he just fire her?"

"Why did he do half the shit he did, Jewel? I don't know."

"Ya'll be having hella shit going on."

"Anyway, the reason why I'm here is because I wanted to see my grandbabies. Since you and Reagan won't bring them to me, I thought I would just come to them."

"You're bored, huh?" he asked laughing at his mother's phony excuse.

"Bored? Jewel, I have entirely too much money to be bored. I'm having my apartment in New York renovated, so I thought I would come and 'hang out' as you would say."

"You went back to New York?"

"Yes, Jewel, I do live there, you know?"

"I know…that's what I'm saying. With everything going on, Reagan wasn't really tryna leave home and go back to Barbados, but me and the boys could have taken a trip for a few days if I had known you were back. They love New York."

"Well, I have other business to tend to out here as well, so just think of it as a dual trip—business and a little family time. Speaking of Reagan, where is she?"

"Your guess is as good as mine," Jewel said pulling out his phone. Still no word from Reagan.

A few minutes later, they heard the front door open, and there she was standing like she'd never left.

"Hey, babe," he said getting up as she walked into the kitchen.

"Hey…I didn't know you would be home," she said before walking over and giving Laura a kiss on the cheek.

"Well, you would have known if you would've answered the phone," he said trying to remain calm. He hated how nonchalant she was about everything.

"I was in Vegas, Jewel. Diamond is getting married, remember?"

"I'm fully aware of that, Rea, but that didn't seem to stop her from calling Sani all weekend to let him know that you were locked up in your hotel room."

"Hey, Laura, how are you?" Reagan asked, not bothering to even respond.

"I'm good, sweetheart. The question is how are you?" she asked with a little concern in her voice. She had to admit that over the last year, Reagan seemed to only be a shell of herself. She didn't really care for Reagan's sake, but she knew how much her son loved her.

"I'll be better once I get my babies home. They're still at Joe's, right?"

"Where else would they be? Diamond's not coming to pick up Jailen until tomorrow."

"Well, I'm about to pick them up tonight then."

"We need to talk, Reagan."

"Can't it wait?"

"No," he snapped, "Every time I try to have a mothafucking conversation with you, you always try to curve a nigga, but fuck that…not tonight."

"Jewel, I'm not about to sit up here and argue with you. We can talk when I get back," she said walking over to the key ring that hung on the wall.

Before she could snatch her keys down, Laura spoke. "Listen, why don't I go pick up the kids?"

"From Joe's?" Reagan and Jewel both asked together.

"Yes, just because we're divorced doesn't mean that we can't be cordial, and plus, I don't have to go to his house. We can meet somewhere. And I've been thinking that since I plan to get a place somewhere around here, I might as well become familiar with the area, no matter how quaint it is."

"But, Mom, you don't drive."

"I'll have my driver take me. That's what I pay them for, right?"

"Laura, you really don't have…," Reagan started.

"I insist, and I won't hear another word otherwise. Obviously, you and Jewel have a few things to discuss, so let me help."

"You sure you gon' be good?" Jewel asked.

"Yes, baby, I'll call your father and have him meet me somewhere nearby. Easy peasy."

"Please, be careful."

"Jewel, I'm not incompetent. I'll be fine," she said grabbing her phone before she walked back upstairs.

"So is that what this is all about, Jewel?" Reagan asked, sitting down on a barstool next to the counter, "You had your mom come all the way out here to fucking babysit me?"

"Shit, somebody needs to, but no, she was here when me and Khailiah got back earlier."

"Khailiah?" she asked smacking her lips.

"Yes, Khailiah…"

All Reagan could do was roll her eyes. "I know that bitch was glad I wasn't here, huh?"

"Uhhhhh…I don't know. I never asked her," he said sarcastically. Reagan and her attitude were really sending him over the edge.

"Yeah, I bet."

"Fuck all that. None of this shit has anything to do with my mom or even Khailiah. It has to do with me and you. What the fuck has been up with you lately? It's like it's either you're not here or you're fucking biting my head off when you are."

"Jewel, I told you that I'm fine. I keep telling everyone that I'm fine," she said putting her head in her hands, "Why can't I just be fine?"

"Because you're not," he yelled.

"You don't know what the fuck I am," she said attempting to get up, but Jewel sat her right back down.

"Listen," he said grabbing her face, trying to calm his words, "I know that losing the baby was hard, but…"

"Hard?" she laughed, "Jewel, you don't know shit because you…were…not…there. I lost our baby alone. I laid on that gurney alone as *our* baby died, and you weren't there."

"Reagan, I've apologized to you more times than there are stars in the sky. What else do you want from me?"

"Nothing," she said shaking her head. He just didn't get it.

"I lost my daughter too, Rea. You don't think I'm not fucked up behind the shit too? I think about her every day. I think about what could've been, but that's not our reality right now. I'm not your enemy though. We should be going through this shit together, not going at each other's throats. I just need you to tell me what you need from me. Tell me how to fix this, Rea, how to fix us."

"I just need you to leave me alone," she said getting up and grabbing her keys from off of the key ring before she was out of the door again.

$$$$$

The Next Morning…

"Good morning, Mr. Sanchez," the lobby's receptionist said as Jewel walked inside.

"What's up, Shaunda? How you doing today?" he smiled.

"Better now that you're here…"

"Don't you have some work you could be doing right now?" Khailiah asked as she rolled her eyes.

"Yo, it's too early in the morning for all that attitude," Jewel said as they walked towards the elevators.

"That bitch is just hella professional…uggghhhh. 'Good morning, Mr. Sanchez,'" she mocked.

"Ay, are you jealous or something, K?" he laughed.

"Get outta here with all that. This is a place of business, and I just think that mothafuckas should act accordingly. That's all."

"Sounds good."

"Look, I'm not 'bout to start with you today. I gotta couple of meetings I need to prep for before 9 a.m."

"Yeah, you go do that," Jewel said walking to his office.

"You need anything before I go?"

"Naw, I'm good."

"I know you're probably gonna get hungry a little later, so I'll have breakfast brought up for you."

"Yeah, make that happen fa sho. I'll have some turkey sausage, a bagel with cream cheese, an orange juice…"

"…and your eggs sunnyside up. Yes, I know, J. You eat that shit almost every day," she smiled, "Oh, yeah, before I forget, Smackz said he was gonna come down and see you."

"At what time?"

"In like fifteen minutes," Khailiah said looking down at her watch, "Get to it, boss."

Jewel walked into his office and couldn't help but to enjoy the view of Downtown Sacramento. It had been a minute since he had been there. With everything going on with Reagan and the business, it seemed like he was never home anymore. Laura insisted that he separate himself from the M.A.C. Boys completely and build his brand from the ground up, but he was the M.A.C. Boys. It ran in his blood. How could he let it go?

Ring. Ring. Ring. Ring. Ring. Ring.

"Hello?" Jewel said sitting down at his desk as he picked up the phone.

"Mr. Sanchez, I have a Stevin Smith on the phone for you."

"Put him through," he said sitting back in his imported, black-leather chair.

"One moment…*BEEP.*"

"Unc…what's hannnnin'?" Jewel sang into the phone.

"Ay, cuz, it's Smackz."

"Nigga, why didn't you just say that?" he laughed.

"'Cause I'm Stevin Smith on paperwork, my nigga. What I look like calling up there and being like, 'ay, can you tell Jewel this is Smackz?' I got way more finesse than that, bruh."

"Yeah, okay, nigga," Jewel laughed again, "What's up with it though? You on your way up here?"

"Naw, something come up at one of the warehouses, so I thought it would be better if I just hit you."

"Everything good?"

"Oh, fa sho, but that's what I wanted to talk to you about. Things have definitely stabilized for the M.A.C. Boys. With all that Kisino bullshit out of the way, our product has been flooding the streets. I don't think there's a corner in Sac that isn't affiliated with the M-A-C right now. You, Sacario, and Hassan are the holy trinity out here. I swear to God."

"Naw, just call me the fucking 'Make-It-Happen Captain.'"

"Shit, I'll call you whatever if we keep bringing money in like this. I'ma need an extra five-hundred of them thangs this month."

"Damn, like that?"

"Straight like that. With Sacario still being in the Bay, we've been able to make our way across that bridge. Now, of course, we still got a lot of work to do, but ain't nobody fucking with us right now. It's only a matter of time before we own Cali."

"You talking my language, cuz. Alright, let me make a few calls, and I'll hit you back."

"One."

Even though Laura and her brother Stevin gave up their distribution rights to Jewel, Hassan, and Sacario, Smackz was more than proud to take his place at the head of the table as the leader of the M.A.C. Boys. He was honored to follow in the footsteps of their fallen uncle, but he had to remain true to himself. He couldn't imagine being stuck in an office all day pretending to be legit. His belonged to the streets, so when Jewel offered him *Sanchez & Associates,* he politely declined. He wanted to be where the action was, and he figured where better to lead the troops than from out of the trenches.

After figuring out the numbers to Smackz's newest request, Jewel picked up the phone.

"Hey, Jewel, what's up?" Khailiah asked.

"Listen, I just got off the phone with Smackz, and he just put in another order for five-hundred."

"Five-hundred, period?"

"No, an extra five-hundred for the month."

"That's big."

"We are on our way, baby," Jewel said grinning from ear-to-ear, "I need you to set up a time for me to meet up with Abuelo."

"For this week?"

"ASAP."

"Okay, I'll let you know what I can find out."

"Yep," he said hanging up, but just as he did, another call came through, "What's up, Shaunda?"

"Mr. Sanchez, someone's here to see you. She says her name's..."

"What's up, brother?" Gabrielle said busting through the door.

"It's good, Shaunda. It's just my sister," he said hanging up the phone.

"Just?" she asked with an attitude.

"What's up, big head?" he asked, pulling her in for a hug, "What you doing down here?"

"I came to talk to the boss man."

"Is that right?"

"Yep."

"What you want now?"

"Don't be like that. I don't just come around when I want something," she said smacking her lips, but Jewel just sat there, "Okay, okay, I need a favor."

"I don't know why you be trying to play me," he laughed, "What is it? You know I got you."

"I want to come and work for you."

"What?" he asked, standing up, "Work for me how?"

"Well, you know I've been helping Keith run *Rich City Cutz* and what not, right?"

"Yeah, how's that going?"

"More than good. He's ready to open up two more locations."

"That's dope."

"With the expansion and everything, I just want to make sure that I'm doing everything I can to help him be successful, you know? Of course, he would never ask for my help, but this shit is all new to him."

"What you need from me?"

"I want you to show me how to wash money."

"Gabby, I…"

"Listen, I know how it sounds, but hear me out," she said grabbing a water from out of the mini-fridge that sat off to the side, "With my business background and the little bit of legal stuff that I picked up from Dad, I know I can be an asset. Keith has a lot of money we can't really do too much with. I know he can put it back into the shop, but I just want to make sure that I'm going 'bout it the right way, and you're a pro at that, my brotha."

"Am I now?"

"Yes! Between all of your rental properties and Reagan's gym franchising, you can't tell me that you aren't out here like a mothafucking wash and fold."

"I don't know, Gabby. Shit can get crazy over this way. We are talking about dope money."

"I'm a big girl, Jewel. Please, just say yes," she said giving him her big, puppy dog eyes.

"Have you talked to Pops about any of this?"

"I mean…not really. You know how he gets."

"Let me think about, okay? I just don't want anything to happen to you, and the closer you are to this shit, that's not something I can guarantee."

"Trust me, okay? I know what I'm doing. I just need a little guidance from my only brother," she said pinching his cheek, "Plus, I would just be a paper-pusher. What could really happen?"

"Let me see what Sacario and Hassan think about it first."

"Perfect! Being that Sacario loves me already, I know I'm in there for sure," she smiled, "Alright, well, I just wanted to put that out in the air, just something for you to think about."

"Well, thank you. It's not like I don't have enough shit on my plate right now."

"Complaints. Complaints. This is what you always wanted, right?"

Jewel couldn't even lie. He was sitting on top of the world, and he never planned on leaving his throne again.

"Where you 'bout to go?"

"To go and pick up Nevaeh from daycare. Keith was supposed to, but he got caught up at the shop. Business has been poppin' lately."

"That's what's up," Jewel said proud of his young nigga.

"Speaking of Keith," Gabrielle said as she made her way towards the door, "Can you not tell him that I came by? I don't want him to feel like I went behind his back or something."

"Look, as long as he doesn't bring it up, I won't, but if he asks me, I'm not 'bout to lie for you, Gabby. Straight up. I love you and everything, but I'm not tryna get in the middle of ya'll shit."

"Thanks for nothing," she said punching him in the arm, "Dad either."

"The same shit applies," he laughed.

"I would do it for you," she smiled.

"Good thing I've never asked you to," he said following behind her as they made their way out of his office.

"Hey…Jewel," Khailiah said catching them before they got onto the elevator, "The food just got here. I was gonna set it up in the conference room."

"I'll be right back," he said before the doors closed in her face.

"Ummmm…who the fuck is that bitch?" Gabrielle asked, doing her best 'Joi' impression from *Friday.*

"Who...Khailiah?"

"I guess," she said as the elevator dropped.

"She's like my assistant."

"Like your assistant, or she is your assistant?"

"She works for me, Hassan, and Sacario. She helps to keep our schedules straight and shit. As hard as it may seem to believe, it's not that easy running a drug empire, Gabby."

"I'm just saying, ya'll seem pretty chummy for her to be your assistant…or whatever. What…ya'll have breakfast together every day?"

"What? You tryna work for the Feds too?"

"She's bad…I can't even hate," she smiled, "Wait, does Reagan know about her?"

"Bye, Gabby," Jewel said as he walked her outside.

"Okay, okay, I will leave you and your mistress alone."

"Why would you even put that out there into the universe like that?" he asked, shaking his head.

"I'm just playing," she said continuing to laugh, "But I have to admit that it's pretty funny seeing you get all flustered behind another bitch."

"Where'd you park?"

"In the garage."

"Well, you go 'head and handle that, kid. I'll hit you up later," Jewel said pulling her in for a hug again. Just before he let her go, they both heard, *BOP. BOP. BOP. BOP. BOP. BOP. BOP.*

With no time to think, he threw her down onto the concrete behind a parked car as he noticed a black, unmarked Chevy Impala race down the street. Knowing that they were gunning for him, Jewel pulled his gun from out of his waistband and returned the fire, hitting the masked man who was hanging out of the window. Within seconds, the car was gone, but he knew that it would only be a matter of time before they came back.

"Gabby, Gabby, are you alright?" he asked, rushing to be by her side. He couldn't help but to flashback to when she was in the hospital after being shot by Pop's cousin KP. Both times, he knew he was the one to put her in harm's way.

"Yeah," she managed to say.

"You good? Did you get hit?" he asked giving her a once over.

"No, I don't think so," she said feeling over her body, "You good?"

"Yeah, I'm straight," he said keeping his eye on each car that crept by. Luckily, the streets were deserted, but Jewel knew he was going to have to answer for what happened.

“Who the fuck was that?” Gabrielle asked as she tried to stand up, but her legs struggled to support her.

“I have no idea,” he admitted.

Chapter Three

Reagan sat in the middle of her king-sized bed and stared out of the window. She became lost in the view of the City and the water that surrounded her. The silence became intoxicating. After getting into it with Jewel, she decided to take a drive to clear her head. She no idea where she was going. She just knew that she had to get away. Almost two hours later, she found herself crossing the Bay Bridge into San Francisco, and the cool night's breeze sent a sense of relief over her. For the first time in a long time, she felt like she could breathe again. After driving around for a while, she decided to get a room at the Fairmont. Once she got settled inside the suite, she almost instantly passed out. For the past year, her mind had been going a mile a minute between Jewel accepting his position as distribution for his family and them losing the baby, and nothing she did seemed to slow it down. She felt lost, hopeless. Losing the baby that she and Jewel created together was her breaking point, and the fact that he wasn't there made it even worse. She knew it wasn't his fault, but she still couldn't help but to blame him. She replayed the night she lost their daughter over and over again in her head, hoping, praying that she could've done things differently to save her, but after a while, she just figured it was all a part of God's plan and became numb.

The next morning when she woke up, it felt like any other day. With Jewel's new position within the organization, he was around less and less, leaving Reagan to hold things down on her own. She had to come to terms that this was who he was now, who he had always been. She just didn't think that he would leave her behind in the process.

Ring. Ring. Ring. Ring.

"What's up, girl?" Reagan answered, trying to force a little enthusiasm in her voice. Even though she and Diamond had gotten closer, she hated talking to her about her problems with Jewel.

"Bitch, where you been at?" Diamond questioned.

"You know…around," she said, not wanting to go into details.

"Let me rephrase that. Where are you now? I went to go pick up Jailen from Jewel, and he said that you weren't there."

"I'm in the City."

"Why?"

"I just had to get away for a minute. Me and Jewel got into it, and I just needed to clear my head for a while."

"Yeah, he said he's been trying to call you…"

"I blocked his number," Reagan admitted, "I'm just tired of his bullshit."

"So you have no idea what happened then, huh?"

The sound of Diamond's voice put her on edge a little bit. "No, what happened?" she hurried to ask.

"Jewel got shot at…in front of his office building downtown."

"What?"

"Yeah, you know he wouldn't tell me too much, but I talked to Hassan. Apparently, Jewel was walking Gabby to her car, and another car drove past them and opened fire."

"Are you fucking kidding me?" Reagan asked as she sat straight up.

"Luckily, no one was hurt, but still, that shit is hella scary."

"I gotta get home," she mumbled to herself, "Ay, girl let me call you back, okay?"

"Okay," Diamond said hanging up.

As much as she and Jewel hadn't been getting along lately, she would have never wanted to see anything bad happen to him. He was her soul mate, and she loved him beyond comprehension. Wanting to finally put their issues aside, Reagan hurried to pack up her stuff before she flew out of the door and headed home.

$$$$$

Jewel sat at his desk going over a few contracts Khailiah needed him to sign. As much as he wanted to be out on the world, he understood the importance of taking care of business first. Golden always tried to remind him of that. With all of his newfound notoriety, the only thing Jewel hoped for more was to stay underneath the radar. He knew what it felt like to be a target, and he never wanted to experience that again.

Ring. Ring. Ring. Ring. Ring. Ring.

"Hello?"

"Mr. Sanchez, Ms. Matthews is here to see you."

"Send her in." After he hung up the phone, Jewel stood up and smoothed out his black Brioni jacket and slacks before he walked over to the door. Before she could open it, Jewel beat his invited guest. "What's up, fam?" he asked with his arms opened wide.

"Nice to see you too," Vanessa smiled, "I just wish you would call me with some good news once in a while."

"You want something to drink or anything?" he asked, closing the door behind her.

"No, I'm good right now. What's up though?" she asked as she sat down in the chair facing Jewel.

"I know you heard about what happened," he started.

"Yeah, I heard a little something, but why don't you fill me in?" she asked crossing her legs.

"It's like I told you over the phone. Somebody tried to pop me right outside the building."

"But why?"

"That's what I pay you for, Nessa. If I knew, those niggas wouldn't be breathing right now."

After Allyn Roberts was murdered, Vanessa was promoted to lead detective of the Sacramento Police Department, and she took her new position very seriously. Being more than familiar with the police, Jewel realized that after everything he had been through, he had to play the game differently this time around, and so did Vanessa. Playing by the rules caused her to lose the love of her life. After Asaya died, she didn't give a fuck about anything anymore, so when Jewel offered her $50,000 a month to be his eyes and ears inside of the system, she didn't see any reason to say no. Vanessa fed Jewel with any information she had about the M.A.C. Boys and made a conscientious effort to keep Sac PD off his ass. Everything had been running smoothly up until now.

"Well, I don't think you have anything to worry about, Jewel. I haven't heard any intel that would suggest that the M.A.C. Boys are on the map again. As far as Sac PD is concerned, you all disbanded the night Kisino Brown was killed. Of course, there needs to be an investigation about the shooting that took place here yesterday, but..."

"But what?"

"But…I took care of it already. I convinced the sergeant that what happened was just a random act of street violence, not gang retaliation."

"And?"

"And the case has been closed. Believe it or not, Jewel, but we have *way* bigger fish to fry."

"Like that?"

"That's what you pay me for, right?" she smiled, "Listen, because no one was hurt, and I know you and Gabrielle aren't going to be too helpful with your witness testimonies, there isn't much to clean up, so relax."

"Speaking of payment," he said opening his desk drawer, pulling out a manila envelope filled with $50,000 cash, "This is for you."

"It's a little early for payment, don't you think?" she asked as she slipped the pack into her purse.

"Naw, it's never too early," he smiled, "Good looking, Vanessa. You have no idea how much I appreciate you."

"You know we gotta stick together," she said standing up, getting ready to leave, "It's what Asaya would've wanted, you know?"

All Jewel could do was hang his head. There wasn't a day that went by where he didn't think about Pop. He wished things could've been different, but he vowed that he would keep his brother's name alive forever.

"How's the baby?" Vanessa asked, "I need to come and see him."

"He's good, getting big as hell. I'll never tell Reagan this, but he looks like Brandon spit him out from the grave," Jewel said shaking his head.

"Asaya would've loved that…" A few moments of silence passed between them as they thought about the loved ones they'd loss. They say, "Time heals all wounds," but it never got any easier for either of them. "Well, let me get out of here. I'll hit you if I hear anything. I doubt I will though."

"Be good," Jewel said kissing her in the middle of her forehead.

"Bye, Jewel," she said as she walked out of his office.

$$$$$

"What's up, Vanessa?" Sacario asked as he, Hassan, and K-2 passed her in the hall, "You here to see, Jewel?"

"I was actually just leaving. I'll see ya'll later though," she said continuing to make her way towards the elevators, "Be safe."

"This nigga," Sacario whispered to himself as they walked right into Jewel's office, not even bothering to knock.

"What are you niggas doing here?" he asked, looking up as they all came in and had a seat.

"You would know if you answered your fucking phone sometimes," K-2 snapped.

"My bad, bruh, I had my shit on silent," he said picking up his phone from off of his desk to see that he had missed calls from Sacario, K-2, and Reagan.

I'll hit her back later, he thought, still mad about her disappearing act.

"What's up though?"

"When were you gonna tell me that Gabrielle almost got popped right outside, nigga?"

"Listen, K, I know how it looks, but…"

"Don't 'listen, K' me. That's my fucking girl, bruh. I think I have the right to know."

"And you do," Jewel said standing up, "But you're acting like I wanted the shit to happen or something. I almost got hit too."

"That's why Vanessa was here?" Sacario asked.

"Yeah," he admitted.

"So the situation is all bad then, huh?"

"I'm not saying all that. I honestly don't know what to think. Gabby came to link up with me right quick. When we got done, I walked her outside to her car to make sure she made it safe, but before we even made it across the street, a nigga let off a round. Instantly, I pushed her down to the ground and started bustin' back. I hit one of the dudes, but they all had masks on, and the car was unmarked. I don't know who the fuck was behind it."

"What did Gabby come to talk to you about?" K-2 questioned.

"Man…," Jewel said not wanting to get in the middle of their relationship.

"Nigga, you better tell me something," he said through his teeth.

"She wants to come and work for me," he admitted.

"What?" The words didn't register. K-2 made more than enough money to take care of Gabrielle and all of her expensive habits, so he didn't understand her request.

"She said she wants to learn how to do the books."

"You told her no, right?"

"I told her that I would think about it…"

"Man, ya'll gon' have to deal with this Gabby bullshit later. K, not to be disrespectful or anything, but I really don't give a fuck about her looking for a summer job right now. You know these nigga weren't looking for her, so the question becomes who's tryna take Jewel's head off?"

Knowing that it was a losing battle, K-2 sat back, but he promised himself that the conversation wasn't over between him and Gabrielle.

"In this line of work, it's not too farfetched to think that you would run into a few enemies here and there," Jewel said.

"Yeah, I get that, but the question is still who? It's been almost two years since all that Kisino shit went down, and we haven't seen an opp 'til now."

"I'm on it, Sacario. I'll figure this shit out. I mean, I have to especially with Smacks increasing inventory by five-hundred packs a month. I really don't have time for this bullshit. Trust me."

$$$$$

Later that night, Khailiah went home with Jewel to make sure he had everything he needed for his trip to see his grandfather. He was scheduled to leave for the Dominican Republic in two days, and she planned to be by his side every step of the way.

"You hungry?" she asked as they walked through the front door.

"Naw, I'm good right now. You?"

"Yeah, I could eat, but I'll just wait 'til I go home."

"You sure? We can order something if you…" Jewel stopped mid-sentence when he saw Laura and Joe sitting on the couch together like an episode of *Family Matters.*

"What's all this?"

As soon as they saw him come in, they quickly scooted almost a foot away from each other.

"Your father brought Chase home," Laura said.

"But I needed to talk to you too," Joe chimed in.

"About what?"

"Sit down, Jewel."

"Khailiah, that will be all," Laura said before taking a sip of her wine.

"Naw, it's good, Ma. Me and K have some business to take care of for Abuelo. That's why she's here. What's up though?" he asked, sitting down on the couch across from them as Khailiah did the same. From the looks on their faces, he knew the news couldn't be good.

"I talked to Keith, and he let me know what happened with you and Gabby."

"What happened?" Laura asked, completely out of the loop. Jewel was a grown-man, so Joe didn't feel like it was his place to fill her in. He knew his son would when he felt like the time was right.

"I tried to talk to Gabby, but after she got shot the first time, she doesn't really like to talk to me about these kinds of things."

"Shot?"

"Listen, Pops…"

"Jewel Noah Sanchez, I swear if you don't tell me what's going on right this instant, I am going to lose it."

"Me and Gabby were leaving my office, and somebody started shooting at me."

"Are you kidding me?" she asked setting her glass down on the coffee table.

"Does it look like I'm kidding, Mom? I know how it sounds, but me and Gabby are both cool."

"Why was she there in the first place?" Joe asked.

I knew this shit was gon' happen, Jewel thought as he sighed to himself. "She said she wants to come and work for me."

"What?"

"She wants me to teach her how to do the books. She's trying to help K with the expansion of his shop."

"Why didn't she just come to me?"

"Maybe 'cause she knows I have a lot more experience in this area," Jewel smiled.

"Son, this is no laughing matter," Laura said getting angry at his nonchalant attitude, "You could have been killed!"

"I had my thang on me, Ma. I was good, and like I said, Gabby didn't get hit. I pushed her out of the way before the bullets started flying."

"Do you think this is a game, Jewel? You are in a very different position than you were before. You have a lot on your shoulders. I need you to take this a little more seriously."

"There's nothing that I take more serious, Ma. I'ma handle it. I'm meeting up with Abuelo in two days. The business is still running how it should be. I haven't missed a step. This was just a small hiccup."

"I don't like this, Jewel. I don't like this one bit. This is how your uncle lost his life. Do you want to end up like Golden, huh?"

"That's never gonna happen."

"I'm pretty sure that's what Goldie used to tell himself too," Laura said shaking her head, "Jewel, I need you to be smarter than this. Your cousin Stevin is more than capable of handling things at the ground level. Let him handle the rift-raft. Your position requires more from you now."

"Mom, I know that, but this works for us. The M.A.C. Boys is who I am, and I'm done running away from that. It's in my blood. Golden showed me a way of life that made me the man I am today, and I'm done apologizing for it. I'm not running away from conflict anymore. That's what almost got me killed the last time. I got this handled."

"Jewel…"

"Mom, there's nothing more to discuss. I know my role as distro puts me on a larger scale, but M-A-C is always where my heart is gonna be. That's where my focus and loyalty is, and nothing or no one can change that."

"Well, if you're not willing to let go of this little hood-fantasy of yours, at least think about getting security."

"I don't need another grown-ass nigga babysitting me. That's out of the question."

"It wasn't a question. I'm not asking you, Jewel. I'm telling you that I'll have it set up by morning."

"Mom…"

"There's nothing else to talk about. You're an investment, and you need to start protecting yourself like one."

"Jewel! Jewel!" Reagan said rushing into the house, "Are you here?"

"I'm in the living room," he yelled back.

Reagan rushed into the living room out of breath but was relieved to know that he was safe until she saw Khailiah sitting a little too close for comfort.

"What's…all this?" she questioned.

"Hey, sweetie," Joe said getting up to give her a kiss on the cheek, "I brought Chase home, but I had to talk to Jewel about a few things."

"Where is Chase?"

"I put him down for a nap maybe like thirty minutes ago," Laura said.

"Hey, Rea," Khailiah said trying to be polite.

"It's Mrs. Sanchez," she said rolling her eyes, "Jewel, can I talk to you please…in private?"

"Yeah," he said following her out into the foyer. He wasn't in the mood to argue, but she had some explaining to do. "Where you been at?"

"I get a call that you were almost gunned down, and here you are playing house with that bitch. Why haven't you been answering your phone?" she asked, completely disregarding his question.

"Who told you I got shot at?"

"Diamond."

"Figures…I had a little situation yesterday, but it's been handled. You would know that if you were here," he snapped.

"So this is my fault now?"

"No, but Khailiah has nothing to do with this shit. I'm so sick and tired of you using her as a fucking excuse."

"What is she doing here then?"

"I got a trip coming up to see my grandfather about a couple things. We came here to work out a few last minute details, but Joe was here, wanting to talk about what happened down at the office 'cause Gabby was there too."

"Is she okay?" Reagan asked softening her tone a little bit.

"Yeah, luckily, neither of us were hurt."

"Listen, I know that things have been rocky between us lately," she said wrapping her arms around his waist, "But I want us to get better."

"I'm not the one who keeps leaving, Rea."

"I know…I know…I was wrong for that, but I needed to clear my head. That's no excuse though. I want us to go back to how things used to be. I'm tired of fighting with you."

"Who you telling?" Jewel said shaking his head.

"Since you're going out to see your grandpa, why don't me and Chase come with you?"

Jewel softly kissed Reagan on the lips and said, "…absolutely not."

"What?"

"No, Rea, I need you to be here with our son. With everything going on right now, the last thing I need is for you to be in the middle of it."

"I thought you said that you have it handled?"

"I do, but that doesn't mean I want you to be all in my shit while I'm handling business. There's a time and place for everything, Rea. You know that."

"So you think that it's just a good idea for you to be traveling by yourself after all this shit?"

"I'm not going by myself."

"What…Sacario and Hassan are coming too?"

"Naw, Khailiah is."

"Excuse me?"

"K's helping me with this deal, so she's coming. What's the problem?"

"Jewel, I'm your fucking wife. That's the problem," she yelled, "I'm so sick of seeing this bitch's face. Ya'll fucking or something?"

"Yo, you buggin' right now," he laughed.

"Jewel?" Khailiah said coming out of the living room.

"What's up, K?" he asked standing in front of Reagan. With her attitude, she was apt to do anything, and he wasn't there for the drama.

"I'ma head home. I see you have a few situations you need to handle," she said looking directly at Reagan, "I'll just email you the itinerary and the quotes I drafted up."

"You should have been done that," Reagan said rolling her eyes, "Bye, bitch."

"Reagan, chill with all that," Jewel said in all seriousness, "I'll walk you out, K."

"Jewel, are you serious?" she asked in complete disbelief.

"Man, I'll be right back," he said closing the front door behind him and Khailiah, leaving Reagan standing all alone.

Feeling defeated and with no energy left to fight, she headed upstairs to check on her son.

Chapter Four

Gabrielle sat on the couch watching *Love & Hip Hop* as her daughter Nevaeh played with her toys beneath her feet. She was in love with her little girl. The moment she gave birth, Gabrielle's world changed for the better. All the things she held to be important no longer mattered anymore. She now lived for her baby, and she was more than happy to dedicate her life to her family. Being with K-2 made her grow up a lot too. She saw how much he had sacrificed just to be with her, and she wanted to do the same, no matter how much he didn't want her to.

"Gabby! Gabby!" she heard him yell as he entered the house.

"Boy, act like you got some fucking home training," she said rolling her eyes as soon as he entered the room.

"Where you been at?" he asked, not in the mood for her mouth.

"At my parents'. After I picked up Nevaeh, I drove to Sac so they could see her."

"You mean back to Sac, right?"

"What?"

"You mean after you picked up Nevaeh, you drove back to Sac?"

"I..."

"Gabby, please don't fix your mouth and try to lie to me," he said swiping his hand over his face in frustration, "I already know what happened."

"You talked to Jewel?" she asked, smacking her lips. *I swear that nigga can't hold water.*

"You damn right I talked to the nigga, but I wanna hear it from you."

"Hear what?"

"Why you were there."

"I went to see my brother if that's okay with you."

"Oh, he's your brother now, huh?" K-2 asked, sitting down on the brown-suede ottoman that sat right across from her.

"What's that supposed to mean?" Gabrielle asked folding her arms across her chest.

"You're only concerned with what Jewel can do for you. I've never seen you so concerned any other time."

"Fuck you, Keith. I don't need to be on his dick to prove to you that that's family. You sound stupid," she spat.

"So why were you there?" he repeated.

"I had to talk to him about a few things."

"About what?" K-2 yelled. He was tired of the back and forth exchange.

"If you must know, I asked him about some business shit."

"*My* business shit, right?"

"*Our* business. Get it right, nigga," she said sucking her teeth.

"See, this is my fault," he said, standing up and smoothing out his jeans, "By letting you help with the shop and everything, I let you believe that we're partners or something."

"Oh, we're not?" she laughed.

"Fuck no! That's my shit. It was *my* idea, *my* money that built the shop, and *my* hands that cut these niggas' hair. What the fuck do you do?"

"Keep that mothafucka afloat," she said in disbelief. She knew that legally she had no claim on K-2's shop, but she believed that they were in this together, but maybe she was wrong.

"You asking Jewel for advice about my shit without consulting me was a complete violation. If I needed help, I would've asked him myself."

"No, you wouldn't," she mumbled.

"What?"

"I said, 'fuck you,'" she said grabbing Nevaeh and heading towards the nursery, but the drama continued.

"Yeah, it can be 'fuck me' all day, but I bet you won't do that cat-ass shit again. I promise you won't."

"Is that a threat, Keith?"

"Man…you heard what I said, Gabrielle. Stay the fuck out of my business."

"Or what?" she asked, stopping in her tracks.

"Or there are gonna be problems."

"You know what?" she asked, laughing again, "I find it funny that you have no problem with me doing all the administrative stuff for the shop when yo' simple-ass pretends like you can't even draft an email, but the moment I start making boss moves on my own, it's all bad? We have all this fucking money that we can't do shit with." After putting Nevaeh in her crib, Gabrielle went into their guestroom, and one-by-one, she began to pull out duffle bag after duffle bag filled with wrinkled $20s, $50s, and $100s from out of the closet. You have like almost $1 million just sitting here. What if the house burned down? Then what?"

"Any other bitch would be happy to be taken care of," he said not seeing her point. All she could do was shake her head.

"Watch the baby," she said flying out of the bedroom and snatching her purse from off of the kitchen counter.

"Where are you going?" he barked.

"Out!" she said slamming the door behind her.

$$$$$

Gabrielle was heated as she merged onto the freeway. She knew that K-2 just wanted to protect her, but she hated how he went about everything. His overbearing attitude was suffocating sometimes, but she loved him. They were a team. As much as she wanted to take the lead on a lot of things, she understood that K-2 loved to provide for his family. She knew they still had to come up with a plan for all the money he had bagged up and just sitting around, but she didn't want to do it behind his back. There had to be a better way.

What was supposed to be a car ride to cool off quickly turned into a short road trip. Before Gabrielle knew it, she was pulling up in front of Jewel's house. She never understood guys but especially guys like him and K-2. She needed a little insight from her big brother, and she knew Jewel could give her just that. After parking along the street, she got out of her car and began to walk up the small flight of stairs that led to Jewel's front door when she noticed her father's Prius parked in the driveway.

"What is he doing here so late?" she asked out loud as she looked down at her phone. It was going on midnight. When she got to the door, she realized that it was unlocked, so she decided to let herself in.

"Jewel?" she yelled, but there was no answer as darkness surrounded her. All the lights in the house were off, so she assumed that no one was home. Just as she was about to turn around to leave, she saw a small glow flicker against the wall in the hallway that led to Jewel's guestroom.

"Jewel? You in here?" she asked again but still there was no response.

Letting curiosity get the best of her, she followed the light down the hall. "Jewel?" Just before she reached the end of it, she could see her father in bed with Laura as they continued to lay soft and seductive kisses all over each other, letting the candlelight dance off their bodies. Gabrielle felt sick to her stomach as she briefly watched her dad hold Laura like she could only assume he held her own mother. Oblivious to her presence, champagne continued to flow as soft jazz played in the background drowning out the world for the both of them. Despite being past lovers, they explored each other with no hesitation. Time stood still for Laura and Joe as they became reacquainted. Even though the years had put distance between them, their love felt the same.

"Dad?" Gabrielle managed to say as she couldn't help but watch her father's infidelity unfold right in front of her eyes.

When Joe looked up, it was like he had seen a ghost. All of the color left his face as the pain and confusion in Gabrielle's eyes penetrated him. He wanted to run after her as he watched her fly down the hallway, but his lack of clothes held him prisoner.

"Go after her, Joe," Laura insisted as she slipped her white, silk robe on, "It's time for her to know the truth," but it was too late. Gabrielle had retraced her steps back to her car through the darkness, leaving the front door wide open behind her.

$$$$$

Two Days Later…

"Jewel, are you sure we can't just stay at a hotel?" Khailiah whispered as they sat in a small boat crossing the waters that led to his grandfather's estate. He remembered his first time traveling with his father to the Dominican Republic. He had to admit back then he was scared shitless, but over the year he had been going back and forth, he seemed to have gotten used to it. Khailiah couldn't say the same though. "With all that money Abuelo has, he could invest into something more stable at least," she said gripping the sides of the boat.

"Es tradición," Luis Miguel, Joseph Sr.'s right-hand man chimed in.

"No se ocupara de sus," Jewel said, "It's cool, K. We're almost there."

Twenty minutes later, they pulled up on shore. Khailiah grabbed her beige Hermès bag as she firmly planted her feet in the rich, brown soil.

"You good, mami?" Luis asked laughing as he smoothed out his black Stanley Korshak suit.

"Yeah, I'm fine now," she said rolling her eyes. As much as she loved being with Jewel and being by his side, she didn't think that she would ever get used to his grandfather's antiquated ways.

"Vamos then!" he said leading them up to the compound.

Over the past year, Jewel and his grandfather had gotten very close. Putting the past behind them, they vowed to never let any more time escape. Jewel was in awe of Joseph Sr. He was such a reserved and humble man, yet he sat on more money than Jewel could even imagine. He wanted to soak up every ounce of game he could, so when Joseph Sr. spoke, Jewel listened, and he didn't mind crossing murky waters to do so. Khailiah on the other hand hated traveling to the D.R. Most of the time Sacario and Hassan were in attendance, so it gave her an excuse to not have to be a part of the festivities, but this time, Jewel was dolo.

"Nieto," Joseph Sr. said as he made his way to the front door. He was ecstatic about Jewel's sudden visit.

"What's up, Abuelo?" he asked giving him a hug as he dropped his bags down by his side.

"I'm hanging in there," he said kissing him on the cheek, "Come in."

As Khailiah and Jewel followed behind him, Luis instructed the housekeeper to take their bags to the guestrooms.

"So what do I owe this pleasure?" Joseph Sr. asked as he sat outside by the pool filling his half-drunken glass full of white rum.

"Business first, huh?" Jewel laughed, "Well, Abuelo, I know that you probably spoke with Luis already, but one of my lines in Sacramento is ready to increase inventory by five-hundred a month. With this increase, I think…"

"No, about the other thing," he said taking a sip of his rum.

"Oh, right…," Jewel said pulling out a suitcase full of cash, "I have half of it here. The other half will be delivered when we leave. I thought it would be too heavy to try and carry over $15 million on that little-ass boat," Jewel laughed again.

"No, the other thing, Jewel," he said setting his glass down.

"My bad, Abuelo, you gon' have to give me a hint or something. I'm lost."

"I spoke with your father."

"Okay," Jewel said looking between Khailiah, Luis, and Joseph Sr.

"And he told me about the little incident that happened down at your office."

"Oh…that," he said shaking his head.

"Yes, that. What happened?"

"I was walking Gabrielle out to her car. She had come to talk to me about a few things, and the next thing I know, I'm pushing her out of the way 'cause a car that rode past us just started firing."

"And you have no idea who it was?"

"Naw," Jewel said shaking his head, "I honestly haven't really had any problems since that Kisino shit, so your guess is as good as mine."

"This is bad for business, nieto."

"Abuelo, I give you my word that I have everything under control. I have come too far to lose it all behind some no-name niggas just looking for a quick come up."

"So what is your plan?"

"I plan to find out who was behind it."

"How?"

"I have my ears and eyes to the streets as we speak, Abuelo. This isn't my first rodeo."

"Your fake confidence scares me, Jewel. I need you to get your head in the game. You just transported almost $10 million dollars on a plane…"

"A private jet," Jewel corrected.

"Excuse me, on a private jet," Joseph Sr. said rolling his eyes, "Do you think these guys give a fuck about your ojos y oídos? There should be no way that they can get access to you. Do you think that anyone can come across those waters without me knowing first?"

"No."

"Exactly! I have protected myself because I am the head, Jewel. Without me, our whole operation will die. A man can function without his hand, foot, an arm, even a leg, but without the head, he is dead. You are too trusting, nieto," Joseph Sr. said looking directly at Khailiah, "You have to be careful with who you have in your circle. Sometimes, it's those closest to us who try to take us out, and we don't even realize it."

"Well, what do you suggest I do?"

"Go get some rest. I know the trip over here must've been exhausting. We'll have dinner around 8 p.m. If you need anything in the meantime, just let Maria know," he said lighting a cigar and blowing smoke rings into the humid air.

$$$$$

After resting for a few hours and washing the jungle smell from off of their bodies, Jewel and Khailiah made their way downstairs to join Joseph Sr. for dinner. He had arranged the meal to be held outside in his garden, so they decided to keep it casual. Jewel opted for a dark-blue sport coat, a white button-up, khakis, and blue Gucci loafers, and Khailiah wore a light champagne-colored lace sundress and strappy sandals. The weather was perfect, and the food smelled even more amazing. She felt like she was finally in paradise as she admired the Bayahíbe roses and Isabel Segundas that led to the table.

"You hungry, nieto?" Joseph Sr. asked, slowly standing up as they made their way across the grass.

"I haven't ate since this morning, Abuelo, so you know this is right on time."

"Perfecto," he smiled, "Teresa has put together a wonderful menu for us tonight."

"What are we having?" Khailiah asked as Jewel pulled out her seat for her.

"La bandera, tostones, pollo croquetas, asopao, chivo guisado, y chenchén," Joseph Sr. said proudly.

"What is all that?" Khailiah asked, screwing her face up.

"Hella good-ass food," Jewel smiled, "Teresa is a beast in the kitchen."

"Khailiah, I promise that you will enjoy the local cuisine here. All of the animals and vegetables are raised and grown right here on the compound, none of that GMO stuff you all have in the states."

"Abuelo, you didn't have to do all this. I would've been fine with some pica pollo," Jewel said.

"What's that?" Khailiah asked again.

"Some fried chicken," he laughed.

"Jewel, don't be silly. It's rare that I am able to feed my grandson. Let me enjoy this."

"Of course, Abuelo," he said not mentioning another word about it.

"Now, while we wait, I thought that we should talk," Joseph Sr. said taking a sip of the ice cold rum that sat right in front of him, "I thought about what you asked me earlier."

"And?" Jewel asked as he scooted to the edge of his seat. Whatever his grandfather said was like gospel in his mind.

"You are a very sweet boy, Jewel. Believe it or not, it's one of the many qualities you've received from your father, but it's time to let that go."

"How though? I only know how to be myself."

"Yes, in some ways, you're right, but in many others, you couldn't be any further from the truth. As you know, when you were growing up, your mother and father had a lot of problems, some that were avoidable and others that were not. With you being an only child, this put you in a very precarious situation. You wanted nothing more than for them to love you and show you that love, so you wouldn't go against anything that they said. Whatever they asked of you, you did because you wanted to make them happy, but that only did one thing, Jewel. That only made you unhappy. While it was not ideal for you to leave home at such a young age with barely any guidance, you took your life back and started living for yourself despite the consequences. Look where you are now, Jewel," Joseph Sr. said pointing around his compound, "This all will belong to you one day, nieto. You have to trust your instinct and never second guess yourself. Even if you are wrong, never second guess yourself. You need to be able to sharpen your intuition."

"I hear what you're saying, Abuelo," he said as he watched the server bring out the first dish filled with white rice, stewed beans, and roasted goat along with a pitcher of passion fruit juice, "but that's what I've been doing. Shit, at least in my mind, I have."

"No," Joseph Sr. said slamming his fist down on the table causing it to shake, "You have been playing, cómo se dice…'kumbaya' with everyone around you. I get that brotherhood means everything to you, and I respect that, but you can't let the loyalty you have towards your friends handicap you. You still have to be a leader, Jewel."

"I am that," he said with confidence. Despite how everyone else felt around him, Jewel was completely confident in his abilities to lead. He had a job to do, and this time, nothing was going to get in the way of that.

"That's what I want to hear. The next time we speak, I want you to tell me that you have someone's head on a fucking stick for this infraction, Jewel."

"You have my word, Abuelo."

$$$$$

Later That Night…

After dinner, Jewel decided to head to bed early. He was far from tired, but his grandfather's words continued to run through his head. He tried to go through his mental rolodex of potential opps, but each time, he came up with nothing. He had to get to the bottom of it.

Who the fuck could it be? he thought to himself.

"Jewel?" he heard Khailiah say from out of the darkness.

"Yeah?"

"You sleep?"

"Naw, you can come in," he said sitting up a little, "You good?"

"Yeah, everything's fine. I just couldn't sleep. It's hot as fuck out here."

"What did you expect? We're in the tropics, baby," he laughed.

"*And* there's no TV in my room. You know I was too poonded to go to sleep."

"I don't think this nigga has any TVs up in this mothafucka. As much as he's here, you would think he would have at least one."

"He has too much money to be sitting around watching TV all day," she said sitting down at the foot of the bed.

"Yeah, I guess…but we head back soon. I know you can't live without that *Housewives* bullshit."

"Don't talk about my shows," Khailiah said softly punching him in his arm, "but forreal, I just wanted to let you know how much I appreciate you bringing me out here. I know with things being so rocky with Reagan and everything, it couldn't've been easy."

"Let me worry about Reagan, okay?" Jewel said wanting to reassure her. Things between them weren't perfect, but at that moment, he didn't have the energy to even think about it.

"Well, let me worry about this then," she said leaning in and kissing him on the lips. She had dreamt of what he would taste like, what he would feel like, and she felt herself getting lost in his touch as he wrapped his arm around her waist and pulled her into him. Placing her hand on his chest, she slowly laid him back, straddling his lap as she kissed all over his neck and chest.

"I've wanted you from the day I first saw you," she whispered into his ear as her tongue caressed his skin.

Jewel gripped her thighs, running his hands over her smooth butterscotch-colored skin. His dick began to get hard just from the sight of her.

"Do you want me too?" she asked kissing him on the lips again.

As much as he wanted to give into his flesh, Reagan never left his mind. No matter what they went through, there was nothing or nobody that could make him turn his back on her.

"...Khailiah," he said easing her off of him onto the other side of the bed, "I think you are an amazing woman..."

"But..."

"But I can't do this. I'm married, and I love my wife," he said sitting up again, coming back to his senses, "My heart belongs to Reagan, and nothing can change that."

"So even though she does nothing for you and she's never there for you, that's still where you want to be?" she asked, sweeping her hair out of her face.

"I don't know what you want me to say. I mean, I care a lot about you, just not how you want me to," Jewel said putting his head in his hands, "I'm sorry if I made you feel like I was leading you on or something, but I can't..."

"Jewel, it's fine. I get it," Khailiah said getting up and walking back towards her room as tears fell from her eyes every step of the way.

Chapter Five

A Week Later…

"Jewel," Laura yelled upstairs from the foyer.

"Yeah," he yelled back.

"Come downstairs. There's someone I want you to meet."

"Not right now, Ma. I'm supposed to be meeting up with Sacario and Hassan, and I'm already running late as it is."

"Jewel, I wasn't asking," she responded, frustrated, "You can give your own mother five-minutes of your time, can't you?"

Knowing that he wasn't going to get out of the front door without talking to her first, Jewel made his way down the stairs as he continued to tie his tie.

"What is it?" he asked before stopping in his tracks, "…who is this?"

"Jewel, I want to officially introduce you to Tusan Cole, your new Head of Security. Tusan, this is my son Jewel Sanchez."

"Nice ta meet yuh, brudda," Tusan said extending his hand to Jewel. From his slight accent, he could tell that he was from the islands.

"Ay, Ma, can I talk to you right quick?" Jewel asked as he walked into the kitchen, never taking his eyes off the young, light-skinned dread-head.

"What is it, son?" Laura asked as her Valentino shoes clinked against the marble floors.

"Who the fuck is that nigga?"

"I told you. That's Tusan. He did security for me back in Barbados…well, I should say his father did, but after Jovan died,

Tusan graciously stepped in to fill his shoes. He's a very good young man…"

"Why is he here though?"

"You may have thought I was joking around during our last conversation, but I wasn't," she said sitting down at the table, "Even more than you being a commodity right now to our organization, you are my son, and I will do whatever it takes to protect you even if that means putting my life on the line...not literally my life, but you know what I mean."

"He's my age!"

"So?"

"I've gone thirty years without having security," Jewel struggled to say. He hated that word. It made him feel like a bitch. "And I don't need it now. I'm good," he said heading towards the foyer, ready to give Tusan his walking papers.

"Jewel, Tusan is the best at what he does, and he is here to stay," Laura said folding her arms across her chest, "I'm not asking you to become BFFs with him, but at least give it a chance. He is here to be your extra set of eyes."

"Ma, I told you I don't need…"

"At least until we find out who was behind the shooting, Jewel," she pleaded.

"Alright," he agreed. He had to admit that he was curious himself, "but once we dead all this shit, the nigga can take his ass back to Barbados."

"Deal," she smiled.

$$$$$

As Jewel made his way to the office, Tusan didn't say a word. He was too busy taking in his new surroundings.

"Where you from, bruh?" he asked, attempting to break the ice.

"Saint Lucy."

"You ever been out this way?"

"Naw, dis be mi first time."

"That's what's up…" Realizing that he wasn't going to get much conversation out of him, Jewel went to turn up the radio, hoping the music could drown out the silence that filled the car.

"So wuh happen?"

"With what?"

"De shooting. Ms. Laurie say dah yuh ran in some trouble, so wuh happen? It will mek mi job a lot easier, ya know?"

"Well, like you probably already heard, I was walking my little sister out to her car when another car rolled past us and opened fire. Luckily, no one was hurt."

"Yeah, dah is lucky."

"But I hit the nigga who was shooting, so I guess it wasn't all in vain, feel me?"

"And yuh in know who it was?"

"Not a clue, but that's what you're here for, right?"

"Exactly. Mi promise we gine tek care of de muddafuckas who did dis. Ya mom is a very special part of mi family, so de least mi can do fuh her is ta look out fuh hers."

"Good looking, bruh," Jewel said pulling up in front of his office, "What's the plan though?"

"Fuh de first few days, I jes wanna see how yuh operate. Where do yuh go, wuh do yuh do pun a normal basis, ya know? Once mi get ya routine down, it will be easier fuh mi ta see if anyting is outta place."

"Right on," he said pulling up to the front door, "I'ma let you out right here. The parking lot is across the street. It should just take me a few minutes to park."

"Jewel, mi jes say dah I need ta follow yuh 'round," Tusan laughed, "Yuh tryna get ridda me already?"

"Naw, nothing like that," he admitted, "To keep it all the way solid with you, I need to call my wife. We had a fight the other day, so you know how that goes."

"Say no mo', brudda," Tusan said getting out of the car, "Mi be right out front."

"I'll be back," Jewel said pulling away from the curb as he made his way into the parking garage across the street.

For a Monday morning, it was packed as usual, but Jewel knew he could count on his reserved spot that sat all the way at the top. Once he pulled into the parking space, he leaned his chair back a little more and grabbed his phone from out of the middle console. It had been a week, and he hadn't heard from Reagan. When he got back home, there was no sight of her or Chase, and she wasn't answering any of his calls. He would've been beating down doors by now looking for her if it wasn't for Sacario. As soon as Reagan arrived at his house with Chase in her arms, he was on the phone with Jewel, letting him know that she had made herself at home in their guesthouse. Not wanting to make the situation any worse than what it already was, he had no choice but to fall back.

Jewel looked up at the ceiling as he waited for Reagan to answer, but as usual, it went straight to voicemail.

"Reagan," he sighed, "I know you see me calling…again, but if not, I know you at least been getting my messages. I know we have some things to talk about, but I don't see how we can do that through your fucking voicemail." Rubbing his hand over his face, he took a deep breath, trying to calm his tone. "I know we have a lot to get through, babe. Please just call me back. I miss you. I miss my son. I know we can get through whatever this is, Rea. I just need you to meet me halfway. I love you," he said hanging up.

Jewel felt lost. Between his problems with Reagan and dealing with an unknown opp, he didn't know which way was up, but he knew he had to remain focused. Dwelling on his personal problems when there was business to handle always got him into trouble. *Not this time,* he thought to himself as he got out of the car. Being distro for the M.A.C. Boys put him in a position where he needed to be. There was too much on the line, and he refused to risk it. Putting himself back into business mode, Jewel made his way to the elevators, ready to get his meeting with Sacario and Hassan started. Just as the doors opened and he was about to walk inside, his phone vibrated in his pocket. Hoping, praying, and wishing that it was Reagan calling him back, he hurried to answer but was quickly disappointed to see that it wasn't her.

"Hello?"

"Hey…"

"…hey."

It had been over a week since Jewel had heard from Khailiah. After denying her advances in D.R., he was surprised to find out that she had left that very next morning. He cared about her, but he refused to put himself in a position to jeopardize his marriage and lose Reagan for good. They had been to hell and back just to be together. Reagan was his sanctuary, and, unfortunately, Khailiah couldn't compete with that.

"I'm glad to see that you didn't lose my number," he laughed, "I was starting to get worried."

"Listen, Jewel, I was just calling to let you know that I'm not coming in today," she said ignoring the pretend banter.

"So…what, you quit?"

"…no. I just need a couple days to get my head together. It's not every day that a bad bitch like me gets flat-out rejected."

"K, don't do that. I didn't reject you because I'm not diggin' you. I'm married with two kids. I'm just not in that space anymore. Why would you want to be the other woman anyway? You don't seem like the 'side-chick' type. You deserve to have a nigga of your own, but unfortunately, that's not me, ma."

"Let's just drop it, okay? We never have to talk about it again. That was a mistake on my part, and I'm sorry. It was completely unprofessional. I'll see you next week or something," she said hanging up before he could say another word.

It just ain't my day, he thought, shaking his head as he made his way across the street.

"Everyting good?" Tusan asked as Jewel walked up.

"More than good," he smiled, "Now, let's get down to business."

"Good morning, Mr. Sanchez," Shaunda said standing up, unable to tear her eyes off Tusan. From his golden, sun-kissed skin, shoulder-length, neatly twisted dreads, and 6'4 frame, all she could think about was mounting him. "Who's this fine gentleman?"

"This is Tusan. He's in security. You'll be seeing a lot more of him around here," Jewel winked. He was just happy to get her attention off him for a change.

As they rode the elevator up to Jewel's office, Tusan remained quiet, but Jewel was determined to break him. If he was going to be around, he had to open up more.

"I see you're gonna fit right in," he spoke up.

"Why yuh say dah?"

"The ladies love you too," he laughed.

"Mi do a'ight, but dah's not mi focus."

"You got a girl back home?"

"Naw, mi no need a woman. Like mi say befo', mi focus right now," Tusan admitted.

"I feel it, bruh. Less of a headache, you know?"

Ding.

As soon as the elevator doors opened, Jewel made his way to his office. He knew he was late for the meeting he had scheduled, but this time, he had a reason.

"Well, there he is," Sacario said standing up as Jewel walked in, "Nigga, you said be here at 9 a.m. It's 9:45 a.m."

"My bad…my bad, I had a few things to handle," he said as Tusan walked in behind him.

"Yo, who is this?" Sacario asked looking suspiciously.

"This is Tusan, our new security detail," he said, not wanting to go into any specifics. He felt stupid enough already.

"What, we need a babysitter now?" Hassan laughed, "Shit must be bad."

"Mi assure yuh, brudda, mi only here ta mek sure dah tings continue ta run smoothly fuh yuh all…"

"Where you from, bruh?" Sacario questioned, noticing his accent.

"Barbados."

"Oh, okay…that's what's up," he said sitting down, "So it's just you?"

"Naw, mi have ten guys pun mi team, but dey will be intraduced lata. Right now, I jes wanna getta feel fuh ya every day, ya know? Pratend mi no even here."

No problem, Sacario thought. "So what's good, Jewel? How'd the trip go?"

"It went cool. I talked to my grandfather, and he made me think about a lot of shit."

"Like what?"

"I've always tried to keep shit cool 'cause to me, there's enough money out here for everybody to eat. I still feel like that, but for as long as I've been in the game, I've finally realized that not all niggas see it the same way. I love ya'll like my own blood, but I've given my loyalty to a bunch of mothafuckas who didn't deserve it, who never did, but I'm not 'bout that life no more. Whoever tried to take me out was gunnin' for me, so it's war now."

"What does that mean though?" Hassan asked.

"The extra five-hundred packs that Smackz wanted is good to go. He should have received the shipment by now."

"I'll check in with him," Hassan said, "I'm supposed to be meeting up with him at the warehouse tomorrow."

"Smackz?" Tusan asked.

"Yeah, that's my cousin. He runs the M.A.C. Boys, so he's in charge of the product."

"He meetin' us here taday?"

"Naw," Jewel said.

"Well, I need ta meet up wit' him wheneva yuh get de chance."

"Why don't you go with Hassan tomorrow?" he asked, wanting to get him out of the way.

"Only if it's okay…," Tusan said looking over at Hassan.

"Yeah, it's good, blood."

"Now with that done, I feel like I can focus on finding out who the niggas are behind the masks and what the fuck they want. I can't sit on this."

"You know we in this together, bruh," Sacario said giving him dap, "Whoever these niggas are will be on our asses next fa sho if we don't move quick."

"We on the same page then," Jewel said, "We have our families to think about, feel me? I can't do that 'sit back and wait' approach this time."

"I'll line up a few hittas," Sacario said, "and you just tell me when. Niggas should know by now not to fuck with the M.A.C. Boys."

"I guess it's time to remind them why that is," he smiled.

"...now that we got all that established, you can tell us what's really going on."

"What you mean?"

"What happened in D.R.?" Hassan asked. Jewel sat back with a blank look on his face. "Nigga, if I'm not mistaken, your wife is currently at this nigga's house, and from what I saw, it doesn't look like she has any intention of coming home any time soon. You finally fucked Khailiah, huh? I knew a nigga couldn't hold out forever," he laughed.

"Yeah, what's going on with that shit, bruh?" Sacario questioned, "I haven't really seen her around the office lately."

Knock. Knock. Knock. Knock.

"Hold that thought," Jewel said hurrying to get up and open the door. Talking about Khailiah and their situation was the last thing he wanted to do.

"I tried to stop him, but he said it was an emergency," Shaunda said out of breath as soon as he opened the door. Just as the words left her mouth, a young, dark-skinned guy rushed past her.

"Can I help you?" Jewel asked taking a step back, trying to place the dude's face.

"You're Jewel, right? Jewel Sanchez?"

"Who's asking?"

"Man, I don't mean any harm by stopping by like this, but I really need to holla at you."

"Ay, who are you, homie?" Sacario asked standing up. He couldn't help but feel like he knew him from somewhere.

"Is there somewhere we can talk in private?"

"Naw, it's good. We can talk right here," Jewel said closing the door on Shaunda who was trying to be nosey, "What's up?"

"Maybe this will remind you," the guy said lifting up his shirt and turning around. Jewel couldn't help but notice the torn flesh that surrounded what appeared to be healed battle scars. "I think this is your work, bruh bruh," he said before pulling down his shirt.

"What?" Jewel asked, screwing up his face,

"My name is Dash…"

"Dash?"

"I know you probably don't remember me, but I could never forget you, blood."

"Yo, who the fuck is this nigga?" Hassan snapped, irritated by the back and forth.

"Like almost two years ago," Dash started, "you and Pop ran up on me and my boys off Valley Hi and lit that mothafucka up."

"Pop?" Jewel froze at the sound of his fallen brother's name.

"You killed my niggas Tone and Mark, but me and my boy Robbie managed to escape with our lives…well, barely."

As Dash continued to speak, it finally hit Sacario where he knew him from.

"Ay, blood, this nigga worked for Kisino…" Before he could finish, Tusan flew over to Dash, grabbed him around his throat, and jammed a pistol against his right temple.

"Jewel, jes tell mi wen," he said through his teeth.

"Yo, yo, yo, I didn't come here for all that," Dash yelled.

"Let him go," Jewel ordered. He was curious about Dash's sudden presence and wanted to hear him out. "What are you doing here?"

Rubbing his neck, he said, "I know how this looks. Yes, I used to work for Kisino and GBM, but for obvious reasons, you know that that's not the case anymore."

"What are you doing here though?" Sacario asked, remembering the shootout that ended Robbie's life.

"I thought we should talk…"

"About?"

"GMB and how we can be of service to the M.A.C. Boys."

"Man, this gotta be a joke, right?" Sacario asked, laughing as he looked at Jewel.

"Let's hear him out," Jewel said, sitting down at his desk.

"J, are you serious, man?"

"So what do you feel like GMB can offer the M.A.C. Boys at this time?" he asked, ignoring the concern in Sacario's voice.

"I know that back then, it was a war zone. Losing Kisino was one of the best and worst things that happened to the clique. It was good because that nigga was crazy as fuck and was going to eventually lead us all to the grave, but it was the worst thing because we were left out there with no leader, no work, no dough, no opportunities."

"What does this have to do with the M.A.C. Boys?"

"Our bad blood stemmed from the beef Kisino had with you. Obviously, coming here with these bullet holes you put in my back, it's safe to say that I've moved on," he smiled, showing off his perfect white teeth.

"So what do you want?"

"I want us to work together."

"Together?"

"GMB is still alive and well, but we have no direction. I think that we can be of service to you. I have over a hundred and fifty soldiers ready to put in work as we speak…"

"Let me stop you right there," Hassan said, standing up, "We appreciate the offer, but we're good over here, homie."

"Naw, I think Dash may be right," Jewel interrupted, "GMB might be exactly who we've been looking for all along."

Chapter Six

Hassan stepped out of the shower, dripping water onto the floor as steam filled the bathroom. He agreed to let Tusan tag along for the day and was ready to get it over with. With everything going on, he understood why Laura was so concerned, but he wanted to believe that the M.A.C. Boys could still hold their own. He didn't like feeling like he was in the Witness Protection Program, but he, Sacario, and Jewel were in a very different situation now. As easy as it would be to revert back to that street shit, he knew they had to play things smarter this time around.

Staring at himself in the mirror, he was ready to get to work.

Knock. Knock. Knock.

"Yes, babe."

"Hurry up…I need to use the bathroom."

"Girl, you act like there aren't other bathrooms up in the mothafucka," he said washing his face.

"All my stuff is in there though," she whined.

Knowing that she wasn't going to let up, he quickly unlocked the door.

"Happy?" he smiled as she walked inside.

"Thank you," she said grabbing her face wash off of the counter next to the sink, "Where you going anyway?"

"To meet up with Smackz, nosey. I knew you were just tryna see what I was doing."

"Yeah, okay," she said rolling her eyes, "You think you can drop me and Jailen off at the field before you head over there? They changed his practice time to this morning, and I do not feel like driving."

"I would, but I'm riding with somebody. I'm waiting on him now."

"Who…Jewel?" she asked, smacking her lips, "I should have that nigga drop us off. He's been to like three of Jailen's games this whole season. I know ya'll call yourselves being busy and all that, but he needs to put forth more of an effort 'cause I can't keep…"

"Diamond, no, it's not Jewel," he laughed.

"Who is it then? I know Sacario went back home, so…"

"This nigga named Tusan," he said wanting to keep it at that.

"Tusan?"

"Listen, there's some stuff I've been meaning to talk to you about," he said grabbing her around the waist and setting her down on the edge of the counter.

"What is it, Hassan?" Diamond asked nervously. She knew the type of life he led, and if he was anything like Jewel, the news couldn't be good.

"I think we should postpone the wedding…again," he said looking down at the floor. It had been weeks since they were supposed to tie the knot, but every time they got ready to walk down the aisle, Hassan would have a change of heart.

"Do you even want to marry me, Hassan?" she asked folding her arms across her chest, "'cause from where I'm sitting, it just looks like one, big fucking joke to you."

"I wouldn't be here if it was a joke, D. You and Jailen mean the world to me."

"Then what is it? You have no idea how embarrassing it is to have to keep telling my family, 'Oh, it'll be next month for sure' or 'Oh, not this month but next month, we're really gonna do it,'" she said painting a smile on her face, "I feel like an idiot."

"You shouldn't though," he said looking up at her as he sat down on the edge of the tub, "There's nothing more I want in this world than to be able to call you Mrs. Diamond Williams, but…"

"But what, Hassan?" she asked getting frustrated. As much as she was in love with Jewel and sat around waiting for him to realize that he loved her too, she couldn't see herself being in that situation again…not even for Hassan.

"It's just that shit don't feel right."

"What does that mean?"

"Ever since Jewel got popped at, it just made me realize that we're in the big boy league now. Everything I do, everything that I am makes me a target, so just by association alone, you become a target too, and I can't have that. I would never be able to forgive myself if something ever happened to you."

"What does that have to do with us getting married though?"

"Everything! I'm not saying that this would happen, but I mean, it could…"

"What?" she snapped.

"What if we throw this big-ass elaborate wedding, and a nigga tried to come through there bustin'? I'm not tryna have our shit looking like Ft. Knox just for us to get married. I want to enjoy that day with you, with our friends and families, not be looking over my shoulder the entire time."

"You sound hella paranoid right now," Diamond laughed.

"But this is some real shit though. At this point, niggas that we don't even know are out for blood. We gotta stay ready, and I just think that having this big wedding would be too much of a distraction or even an opportunity for some shit to go down. Don't get me wrong, babe, you deserve this wedding and some mo', but as the man of this family, my only job is to make sure ya'll are straight."

"So what's the alternative then?" she asked, jumping off the counter before she stood directly in front of him.

"I've been thinking about that too," Hassan said laying his head softly against her chest as he wrapped his arms around her waist, holding tight to her buns.

"Why don't we just go down to the courthouse?"

"What?" she asked trying to pull herself away, but his grip was too strong.

"Hear me out before you get to trippin'," he laughed, "Even though I want to hold off on all the festivities and shit…at least until we figure all this bullshit out, that doesn't change the fact that I still want you to be my wife. Let's just go down to the courthouse and get all the paperwork out of the way. That way, it can be official, and that will eliminate the pressure of putting on this show for everybody." Ready for Diamond to let him have it, Hassan remained quiet waiting. He knew how much time and energy she had put into planning their wedding, but something in the air didn't feel right. Despite how much he loved her and wanted to make her happy, he couldn't take the chance with her life.

"…okay," she said, kissing him in the middle of his forehead.

"Huh?"

"I said, 'okay.' Let's do it."

"Are you serious?"

"Why you sound all surprised?"

"D, no offense, but you are a little high-maintenance."

"'Spoiled' is probably a better word," she smiled, "Look, I love you, and I know that coming to this decision couldn't have been the easiest for you. I know you're just looking out for us, so I don't want to add to that stress. Honestly, as long as I can wake up every day next to you and be able to call you mine forever, I'm good."

"You know that's why I love you, right?" he asked, standing up as he placed a kiss on her lips.

"I love you," she said kissing him back, "but there's something else we need to talk about."

"Oh, shit," Hassan said rubbing his hand over his face.

"Unlike you, I have good news…well, at least I think it's good news," she said becoming nervous again.

"I need some good news, baby. What is it?"

"Well, you know how I haven't been really feeling too good for the past few weeks?"

"Yeah, the doctor said it was the flu, right?"

"At first…"

"If it's not the flu then what is it?"

"…I'm pregnant," she smiled.

"What?"

"I'm only like three months, but yeah, the doctor confirmed it."

"I'ma be a daddy?" he asked as a smile spread across his face. All she could do was shake her head as she looked into his eyes.

"Are you happy?"

"Come here."

Feeling his dick poke her through his boxers, Diamond already knew what time it was. With one hand, she slid her hand inside and began to stroke him up and down as small moans escaped his lips.

"I want you," she said looking into his eyes.

"Not in here," he said picking her up and taking her back into their room. Luckily, Jailen was still asleep because he needed his fix.

Once they got inside the master bedroom, Hassan locked the door as their tongues continued to intertwine. He struggled for air, but she felt too good to even let himself breathe. Laying her thick frame down on the bed, it didn't take long before his boxers were on the floor and his dick was standing at full-attention. Not needing to be told, Diamond slipped the head into her mouth savoring the taste. As she continued to suck, her spit coated his pipe, making it glisten in the mid-morning sunlight.

"Fuck, that feels good," Hassan said letting his head fall back in ecstasy.

Focused on the mission at hand, she cupped his balls and began to juggle them as the slurping continued.

"Ooooohhhh, you taste so good, baby," she managed to say while keeping her mouth full and looking up at him.

Unable to take it anymore, Hassan laid Diamond down on her back, slipped off the black, lace boy shorts she wore, and dove in face first. Just the smell of her sent him over the edge. As he licked and kissed her middle, Diamond squirmed with pleasure. She ran her fingers through his dreads as he lifted her leg up and threw her thigh over his shoulder, wanting to go deeper. With two fingers, he played with her soaking wet hole while he let his tongue dance over her clit.

"Fuck, baby, I'm 'bout to cum," she yelled.

"Not yet," he said stopping, "I want you to cum on this dick first."

In one swift motion, he turned her over by her hips as she arched her back, laid her chest down, and hiked her ass up in the air. Taking the coconut oil that sat by the bed, Hassan gently massaged her back, butt, and thighs. The glow from her mocha-colored skin drove him crazy.

Waiting for him to enter, Diamond gripped the comforter that sat underneath them, preparing herself for impact. As Hassan slid inside her tight, wet box, all she could do was exhale. Stretching her walls, it didn't take long before he found his rhythm and that pain quickly turned into pleasure.

"Just like that, baby," she said bouncing her ass back against him with every thrust he made. All that could be heard was the sound of skin smacking together as their love filled the room. Needing to go deeper, Hassan picked his right leg up for balance and fucked her harder.

"You about to make me cum like this, baby," he said as he continued to watch her ass bounce up and down on his dick.

"I want it."

"You want it?"

"I want it, daddy," she purred.

That was all Hassan needed to hear before he began to bang her back out. With each movement he made, he went a little faster until he felt his orgasm at the base of his dick. Feeling him about to explode, Diamond tightened her pussy muscles until he couldn't take it anymore. Quickly standing up, he shot hot cum all over her ass and back as she tried to catch her breath. Beating his dick until every drop covered her skin, he stood frozen above her.

"Fuck," he said before jumping off the bed and walking to their bathroom to grab a warm wash-cloth as Diamond patiently waited.

"You must've missed this pussy?" she laughed with her ass still in the air.

"You know I did," Hassan said as he caressed her body with the wet towel, erasing the evidence of his satisfaction, "I need that pussy morning, noon, and night. You know I go crazy without it."

"Uhmmm hmmm…that's how we got into this situation," she said getting up to grab her robe when suddenly Hassan's phone started ringing. Not wanting to mess up the mood, he pretended like he didn't even hear it. "It's okay, Sani. I know it's probably business. I'm 'bout to get in the shower anyway, baby daddy."

"Alright," he said kissing her on the cheek, "I think I like 'Daddy' better though."

Before she walked out of the room, he rubbed the small bump that was starting to form, thankful for all that God was bestowing upon him. He could honestly say that he was blessed.

"I love you," he said as she made her way to the bathroom.

"I love you more."

His phone stopped ringing, but soon, it picked back up again.

Ring. Ring. Ring. Ring. Ring. Ring.

After putting his boxers back on and sitting down on the bed, he answered it.

"Hello?"

"Hassan?"

"Yeah, this him. Who's this?" he asked not recognizing the number.

"Tusan…"

"What's up with you, bruh?"

"Mi jes wanted ta know if yuh still wanted ta do dah ting taday?"

"Oh, fa sho, Smackz knows we're on the way. I'm getting dressed now."

"Okay, good, Mi coming now den."

"Yep, just hit me when you get outside. I'll text you the address," Hassan said before hanging up.

Once he finished texting Tusan the directions to his house, he took his boxers back off and decided to slip into the shower with Diamond. He knew he had to get ready, but he figured he still had time for round two.

$$$$$

After making love again, Diamond was finally able to pull herself away from Hassan just in time to get Jailen to baseball practice. As much as he hated to see her go, he knew he had some business to take care of too.

BEEP. BEEP. BEEEEEEEEP.

Hassan looked out of his front window to see Tusan parked outside in his driveway in a 2016 matte-black Escalade sitting on 26s.

This nigga out here looking like the ghetto Secret Service, he thought to himself as he slipped his hammer in the back of his pants. Even though Tusan was supposed to be acting as security, Hassan could never be too careful.

Putting the last finishing touches on his outfit, he slipped his 24-karat gold rope chains over his all-white Lacoste tee before he was out the door.

"What's up with you, family?" he asked as he walked out towards Tusan's truck.

"Mi good, brudda, ready ta get de day started, ya know?" he smiled a little.

"Good, Smackz is a good dude, very smart. I think that you'll see how he runs the operations for the M.A.C. Boys is more than efficient."

"Leh's hope so," Tusan said pulling out of the driveway, "Ms. Laurie kinda gih mi some background pun de M.A.C. Boys, but wuh's de real deal?"

"I'm the newest member, but I know that Jewel and Sacario have been rocking for years. They've been to hell and back tryna keep the clique together. I don't know all the specifics, but basically Jewel's uncle Golden ran the M.A.C Boys since its inception. Before he died, he passed everything over to Jewel. Jewel was running shit for a while until they got into it with a few opps, and because of that, one of his closest potnahs got done in. From what I heard, he was never the same after that, so he put Sacario in charge. That lasted for maybe a little over a year before Jewel's mom hit him about being distro, and Jewel created this partnership between me, him, and Sacario, leaving Smackz in charge of running the M.A.C. Boys, and the rest is history, feel me?"

"So wuh role does Jewel play now dah he move up?"

"I mean, we act as the sole supplier to the organization, and Jewel is kinda like a big brother to Smackz, like his guidance, you know?"

"It's good dah he is dere. Who knows wuh would happen if he wasn't."

"Yeah," Hassan said looking out of the window.

"Wuh 'bout Smackz den?"

"What about him?"

"I mean, how does one person operate at such a high level?"

"Honestly, he's been doing this shit way before I ever came around. At first, he was just managing one warehouse in Sac, but now, he has about six or seven of them mothafuckas around the city. Like I said, Smackz is very smart. Even though bricks flood those warehouses day and night, very few people get to actually go inside. He has armed soldiers placed all over the area, and the outside of the buildings are covered with cameras. You gotta have a password just to get in, plus, prior authorization from Smackz, but being that I play for the home team, feel me, I can come and go as I please. If you were anybody else though, it's almost impossible to get inside unnoticed. Smackz knows that he has to be on top of shit especially now, or it could cost him his life. He moves entirely too much weight to be careless."

Thirty minutes later, they pulled up to an abandoned-looking building in the industrial area in West Sacramento.

"Ay, pull up behind here," Hassan instructed, making sure the coast was clear, "You ready?"

"Yuh lea', mi follow," Tusan said turning off the ignition.

Hassan got out of the car and walked up to the back door, releasing the latch to a small fuse box and entered a twenty-digit password onto the keypad that sat inside. The front door clicked several times and then slowly opened. Hassan and Tusan walked up a few flights of stairs before they reached another steel-plated door. After ringing the buzzer, Hassan stood in front of a small camera.

"Password?" an unidentified voice asked.

"9-3-5-6-8-1-1-6-5-3-2-4-7-6-1-3-0-9-2-5."

"Who sent you?"

"J. Sanchez," Hassan said staring into the camera.

"Your name?"

"Hassan Williams, and I have a Tusan Cole with me."

"Who are you here to see?"

"Smackz."

"Access granted."

Suddenly, the double doors swung open revealing an all-white room. Tusan was taken aback by how inconspicuous it was. On the outside, the building looked like it hadn't seen anyone in years, but he was impressed by the elaborate drug lab Smackz had managed to create inside. Tusan admired the assembly line full of naked women who cooked, broke down, and packaged drugs of all kinds. It became an art to them.

"Hassan, what's up, bruh?" Smackz asked coming out of the back room.

"How's it shakin', blood?" he asked giving him dap.

"As you can see, shit is A-1," Smackz said motioning around the room at all the cash and product that covered the metal tables that sat against the walls, "You know I can't complain."

"I see, I see," Hassan said smiling, "That extra shipment must've came through."

"Oh, no doubt. Ya'll came through for the kid in the clutch," Smackz said giving him dap again, "Between this place and our other spots, we got like almost $35 million worth of product to distribute."

"You don't think that's too much?"

"If it was just out here, I would say, 'fuck yeah, that's too much,' but between Sacario being out in the Bay and Jewel's connects in LA and Vegas, I think I can get this off pretty easily. I might have to increase our manpower a little bit though..."

"Jewel might have the solution to that problem," Hassan said shaking his head.

"What?"

"Naw, I'll let him fill you in, bruh, 'cause the shit still don't make sense to me."

"Ya'll niggas always got something going on," Smackz said laughing.

"...ay, my bad, blood. This is Tusan, the new Head of Security. Tusan, this is Smackz, leader of the M.A.C. Boys organization."

"Nice ta meet yuh, brudda," Tusan said extending his hand.

"Likewise...so you here 'cause of that shit that happened the other day with Jewel and his sister?"

"Yeah..."

"Auntie Laura wasn't playin', huh?"

"It's fuh everyone's safety really," Tusan said walking around the room.

"I feel it. Jewel needs to find out who's on his head before it's too late. That shit is bad for business."

BOP. BOP. BOP. BOP. BLAT. BLAAAAT. BOP.

"Yo, what the fuck was that?" Hassan asked.

"It sounded like gunshots," Smackz said running over to his security monitors.

"Who the fuck would be bustin' way out here?" he asked confused by the sudden activity.

"These niggas," Smackz said pointing at the screen, revealing ten armed men in all-black laying out the guards who surrounded the building, "Fuck! We're under attack." He tried to run to the back to set off the lock-down feature in the control room, but it was too late. As soon as he left the room, the metal door that led to the lab flew open as a barrage of bullets followed next. The girls who worked for Smackz screamed as they ran every which way looking for a safe place to hide, but their efforts were useless. One by one, the masked gunmen emptied their clips into their exposed flesh, dropping them like flies.

As a natural instinct, Hassan and Tusan both took cover behind a metal table that had been flipped over in the middle of all the chaos. Without saying a word, they both looked at each other, pulled out their guns, and started blasting. Bullets ricocheted off the walls as they all stood in the midst of the crossfire. Tusan made his move to take out one of the unknown intruders, but before he could, Smackz came out of the room letting his gun spray, but he wasn't quick enough. Never seeing it coming, one of the men in black came up from behind him and put a bullet in the back of his head. Hassan watched as his body fell, and from the lifeless look on his face, he knew he was gone.

What the fuck am I gonna tell Jewel? he thought as he hung his head.

At that point, it was either life of death. Ready to go out in a blaze of glory, Hassan fired back, but with everything going on, he couldn't steady his hand.

"Hassan, mi got dis. Yuh gonna get yuhself kill," Tusan yelled. Just as the words left his mouth, Hassan felt like he was on fire as a bullet melted through his skin. He grabbed his right shoulder hoping to stop the blood that started to spill, but nothing was helping. Quickly, his shirt and hand were covered.

Unable to think straight, he began to fade in and out of consciousness, but he watched as Tusan tried to repay the masked men for their sins, but his gun jammed. With no other choice, he jumped behind the table again, put his finger to his lips, and said, "Ssshhhh" as the storm of fire suddenly stopped. Satisfied with their handiwork, the five guys who were inside took everything they could, stuffing money and drugs into the black duffle bags they held in their hands. Knowing better than to try to be a hero, Tusan remained silent until he heard their footsteps going back down the stairs and disappear into nothingness.

Chapter Seven

"Well, looks who's up," Kiko sang as she walked into the kitchen.

"Thanks again for letting me stay here, girl," Reagan said, feeding Chase a bowl of oatmeal.

"You know it's good. We're like family. I'd rather you be here safe and sound with us instead of bouncing from hotel to hotel with the baby."

"Yeah, 'cause you know Jewel be checking the cards tryna track me down and shit."

"Bitch, you act like he can't just pop up over here now," Kiko laughed, "You know Sacario already told him you were here."

"I figured. He's been blowing up my phone all week."

"Rea, you know you my girl and all, and you can stay here for as long as you need to...but are you gonna finally tell me what happened?" she asked taking a bite of toast as she sat down at the kitchen table.

Taking a deep breath, Reagan didn't even know where to begin.

"Me and Jewel are just not on the same page anymore," she sighed.

"Every relationship goes through its ups and downs though, Rea. Remember, it's for better or worse..."

"Well, I don't think the shit can get any worse at this point."

"You guys still arguing about losing the baby?" she asked, putting her head down.

"It's not even that though," Reagan said shaking her head, "I mean, there's nothing we can do about losing the baby. I know that...but Jewel acts like he doesn't even want to be with me anymore."

"Now I know you're lying. Bitch, you know Jewel is *stupid* over you. It's really sickening sometimes."

"He used to be...," she said rolling her eyes.

"What's that supposed to mean?"

"Have you ever met Khailiah Moore?"

"Who...that tramp that calls herself Sacario and Jewel's 'assistant' or whatever?" Kiko asked using air-quotes.

"The one and only," Reagan said rolling her eyes again.

"Yeah, I met the bitch a few times. I never really saw her around Sacario and Hassan all like that, but I can say that she seems to like Jewel a whole lot. You know I was all over that. I caught myself about to check her a couple times, but Sacario keeps insisting that it's all business and that nothing is going on between them. That being my nigga and everything, I wanted to believe him, so I fell back. Plus, I didn't want to make something out of nothing if the shit really is nothing, you know?"

"You were right to be suspicious..."

"They fucking?" Kiko asked, covering her mouth.

"Probably," she said shrugging her shoulders.

"Don't do that, Rea. Jewel would never cheat on you."

"That's what I thought too, but he's been acting hella sus lately. I don't know what else to think." Just even thinking about all their drama exhausted her. "Did Sacario tell you about the trip to D.R.?"

"Yeah, he said Jewel was going dolo though. How'd it go?"

"If by dolo, you mean he went with that bitch, then I guess it went fine."

"He took her out there?"

"Yep, but it's not the first time. I never really had any reason to trip before because Sacario or Hassan would be with him, but not this time," Reagan said smacking her lips, "This time, Ms. Khailiah was right by his side while my ass was stuck at home...well, until I came over here."

"So you weren't there when he got back?"

"Nope."

"How'd he pull that off?"

"Don't get me wrong, he told me up front that he was going with her, but that's my issue. He has no problem parading her in my face like I'm the side-bitch or some shit."

"I just think ya'll need to talk. You may be blowing all this out of proportion."

"Kiko, what would you do if you were in my shoes?"

"Cut a bitch..."

"K, I'm serious," Reagan laughed.

"I am too," she said in all seriousness, "Sacario knows how I get down, and he knows that I don't play that shit. I know he would never disrespect me like that, so that helps eliminate my craziness…just a little bit," she said pinching her fingers together, "I used to have problems with him and other bitches when we were first dating, and all that brought was drama, drama, and more drama. I was out here fighting these hoes like it was my job. It was the principle though, but that shit got old fast. I got to a point where I was over it. I couldn't see myself risking my freedom on a daily basis for a nigga who was willingly entertaining these females. I was in a relationship with him, not them, you know? At the time, we had a little apartment in the East. One night, he came home hella late, and I had all my shit packed and was out the door. Of course, he was begging and pleading, but I was done. We were broken up for like a few months…"

"So what happened?"

"What you think happened?" Kiko asked raising her ring finger, showing off the rock that she proudly wore, "The nigga made his next choice his best choice and got with the winning team, hoe."

"You are crazy," Reagan laughed.

"Naw, but forreal, I'm a very forgiving person, and I understand that we all make mistakes, but what type of woman would I be if I allowed any man to continue making the same mistakes on me over and over again? I may be a lot of shit…but a weak bitch has never been one of them. I'd rather be on my own, and he knows that. All I'm saying, Rea, is that we all have our dark pasts, but that doesn't mean that we can't have a bright future, you know?"

Deep down, Reagan knew that Kiko was right. As she continued to talk, Reagan thought back to when she and Jewel first got together. Everything about their situation started out messy. After being with Styles for over seven years, she never could have imagined that she would let it all go for a complete stranger, but something about Jewel drew her to him. Whenever they were together, she felt at home, at peace, and that soon became a scary and unfamiliar feeling. Not sure if her feelings were based in reality or a desperately needed fantasy, she allowed Brandon to come in and be her distraction. Everything about their situation was toxic. While she was just looking for a quick fling, Brandon was willing to do any and everything to ensure that they stayed together. Reagan being with Brandon broke Jewel's heart as much as he didn't want to admit it. He blindly put his all into her despite everyone telling him to run the other way. He loved her even before he knew why, and there was no way Reagan could deny that. And even though Jewel had a baby outside of their relationship, it was before they even knew of each other's existence, but Reagan couldn't say the same. She had no idea how hard it was for Jewel to look at Chase every day and know that he was taking care of another man's baby, his brother's baby, but as a man, he had no other choice. Despite Reagan's past indiscretions, his love for her allowed him to forgive her and see all of the good they had built together. Maybe it was time for her to do the same.

"...Reagan, Reagan! Are you listening?"

"My bad, girl," she said snapping back from her thoughts, "This nigga got my head all fucked up. I know that I've done more than my fair share of dirt, but I don't know...this shit just feels different."

"It's not like ya'll about to get a divorce or nothing..." Reagan put her head down as the question swirled around in her mind. She never really thought about it. As much as she was mad at Jewel, she loved him more. "Right, Rea?"

Suddenly, the front door swung open, and Sacario flew inside.

"Kiko, Kiko!"

"I'm in here, babe," she yelled back, "What's wrong?" The anxiety in his voice sent chills up her spine.

"I gotta go," he said handing her their daughter Arianna. He had just picked her up from school.

"Sacario, slow the fuck down," Kiko said grabbing his arm before he could run out of the kitchen. When he looked down at her, she could see the sweat that poured from his face.

"Kiko, I don't have time for this," he said snatching away, trying to hide the tears that pooled in his eyes, "I said I gotta go."

His evasiveness was starting to put Reagan on edge as she watched him and Kiko go back and forth. She just prayed that the situation had nothing to do with Jewel.

"Sacario!" Kiko screamed, "Stop and fucking talk to me." Refusing to let him leave the house before saying something, she threw herself in front of the front door.

"Smackz...just got killed, and Hassan got...hit up too," he said moving her out of the way, "I'll call you when I know more."

Before she could respond, he was out the door.

$$$$$

"Gabby, your dad is calling again," K-2 said walking into their bedroom, showing her his phone as it continued to ring, "What do you want me to say *this* time?"

It had been over a week since Joe and Gabrielle had spoken to each other, but she just didn't know that to say. After catching him in bed with Jewel's mother, she felt like everything he had ever told her was a lie…he was a lie. All her life, she admired the relationship that her parents shared, and she vowed that if she ever got married, she wanted her marriage to be just like theirs, but Joe turned out to be just a typical nigga. At almost 20-years old, she never imagined that she would have to question her father's loyalty, but here she was.

"Tell him whatever you wanna tell him," she said rolling her eyes, "He knows I'm not fucking with him."

"I say you call him back," K-2 said opening the blinds, allowing the sunlight to flood the room.

"For what?" she snapped, "What could he possibly have to say to me?"

"You would find out if you just answered the phone," he said sitting down on the bed.

"He's cheating on my mom, Keith…I'm good."

"Yo, I still don't believe that," he laughed.

"It's not fucking funny," she said slapping him upside his head, "And I saw that shit with my own eyes. You're not 'bout to sit here and tell me that I didn't."

"I'm laughing 'cause the shit is wild," he said pulling her in for a hug, "As much as Jewel has told me about Joe and his mom, I just can't believe that he would even take it there."

"Well, believe it, nigga, 'cause it happened," she said laying her head on his shoulder, "And as a matter of fact…fuck Jewel! His bitch-ass was probably in on the shit too."

"Naw, that's not even Jewel's style. I can't see him co-signing nothing like that. He has enough shit going on than to be playing matchmaker with his mama and Joe. He'll probably be just as surprised as you were."

"I doubt it," she said rolling her eyes again, "What am I gonna tell my mama?" Thinking about how much Isabella loved Joe broke Gabrielle's heart. Although they didn't start off their relationship on the best of terms, they had built a wonderful life together and created a beautiful family despite the trials and tribulations they both had to endure. Gabrielle didn't understand how he was willing to throw that all away so easily.

“You’re not ‘bout to tell her shit,” K-2 said lifting her head up by her chin.

“What?”

“That’s not your place, Gabrielle.”

“The fuck it ain’t. My mom has been there for me since day one, and I refuse to let anyone hurt her, not even my own daddy. Do you know what this shit is about to put my family through?”

“I hate to break it to you, babe, but this shit has nothing to do with you. Even though that’s your mom and dad and all, this is between them. They gotta figure this shit out…on their own.”

“So you expect me to just sit back and watch my mama get played? Fuck that!”

“I’m not saying that…just talk to Joe first. This could really be just a big-ass misunderstanding, and you running your mouth could make shit a whole lot worse.”

“I told you…I have nothing to say to that nigga. Drop it!”

Suddenly, the sound of their daughter’s cries could be heard throughout the house.

“You sound hella childish,” he said getting up to tend to his baby girl, “If you’re not gonna talk to Joe, at least talk to Jewel. I know that nigga can help make sense of all this.”

Before Gabrielle could say a word, K-2 was out the door. As much as she didn’t want to admit it, she knew that he was right. If she wanted any answers, she would have to go to the source, and since talking to her father was out of the question, Jewel would have to do.

$$$$$

Two hours later after making sure K-2 and Nevaeh were situated, Gabrielle found herself driving up to Sacramento again. She had made the trip a million and one times before, but this time felt a little different. Her heart pounded with each exit sign she passed. Tempted to take one of them, say, “fuck it,” and turn back around, she knew she couldn’t. She was on a mission.

Once she arrived at Jewel’s house, she double-checked to make sure Joe’s car was nowhere in sight. As much as she had to say to him, she couldn’t face him, not yet. Taking a deep breath, Gabrielle walked up the steps to Jewel’s front door.

It’s now or never, she thought before exhaling.

Before she could knock, she heard Jewel's voice boom through the door.

"Ma, I told you I don't have time for this shit! Didn't you hear what Tusan just said? Smackz is gone…your nephew is gone, Ma. Gone! I gotta go."

"Jewel, I know that a lot is going on right now, all the more reason for you to take Tusan along. Your uncle is on his way out here now. I'll be fine."

"No, there's no time. With you and Jailen here, I would feel more comfortable with him looking over shit here. Hassan is at home with Diamond shot the fuck up. The last thing I need is for Jailen to see any of that shit."

"It's really no problem, Jewel. Mi can have one of mi men come an' keep an eye pun de property. Dere were a lot of dem in dere, brudda. It's not safe fuh yuh ta go pun yuh own."

"I appreciate you, bruh bruh. I really do, but making sure my son's safe is my only priority at this point."

"Mi got yuh. Whateva yuh need. Dah's wuh mi here fuh."

Feeling guilty about being out of town so much lately, Jewel decided to surprise his oldest son at his baseball practice. Diamond was probably more surprised than Jailen was, but she appreciated his effort. She knew how much her son loved Jewel, and as much as they didn't get along, she would never stand in the way of their relationship. After the practice was over, Jewel offered to take Jailen back home with him. Of course, he jumped at the opportunity, so Diamond had no other choice but to let him go. Once they left, she went home preparing for Hassan's arrival. With Jailen gone, she wanted to take advantage of the alone time they had, but when he got there, she saw the last thing she ever expected to see.

"Jewel…," Laura began.

"The nigga's staying here," he barked, "and that's fucking final!"

Tucking his gun inside his waistband, he headed towards the front door when he ran right into Gabrielle who was still standing outside.

"Gabby?" he asked in confusion, "What are you doing here?"

"Is now a bad time?" she asked, not knowing what else to say. The look on his face sent chills up and down her spine.

"Kinda," he said not having time to go over the details, "Ay, I'll hit you later though."

"Jewel, we need to talk," she said before he could walk outside.

"Listen, Gabby, if this is about you coming to work for me, we gon' have to talk about that later. I'ma hit you…I promise," he said making his way to his car.

"It's about your mom fucking my dad…," she yelled after him.

Wanting to make sure he heard her correctly, he slowly made his way back into the house.

"What?" he asked like she was speaking another language.

"Last week, I caught Dad and yo' hoe-ass mama in bed together," Gabrielle said looking directly at Laura.

"Yo," Jewel said wiping his hand over his face, "As much as I want to know what you're talking about right now, I don't have time for this *Days of Our Lives* bullshit. Hassan got shot today. Everything else is irrelevant to me. I'll hit you later," he said leaving for good.

CLAP. CLAP. CLAP. CLAP. CLAP.

Laura stood behind Gabrielle slow-clapping as she turned around.

"You feel better, little girl?" she smiled.

"What the fuck is that supposed to mean?"

"What did you think Jewel was gonna do? Punish me?" she laughed.

"I needed to know if he knew," she admitted.

"Well, I'll be the first one to tell you that he didn't. No one did."

"Since you're in such a telling mood, Laura, why don't you tell me what the fuck is going on?" Gabrielle asked as she crossed her arms across her chest.

Seeing the tension brewing in the air, Tusan decided to excuse himself. "Ay, Ms. Laurie, mi be in de back if yuh need mi," he said walking towards the kitchen.

"Okay, sweetheart," she said never taking her eyes off of Gabrielle.

"I'm a big girl, Laura. I can handle it."

"You sure?"

"Try me…"

"So you want to know what's going on between me and your father, huh?" Laura said more to herself, "…we're just having fun."

"Fun?" Gabrielle snapped, "You think it's fun fucking on a married man?"

"Your mother did," she winked, "Let's not forget that I was the *original* Mrs. Sanchez."

"That was then…this is now," Gabrielle said not wanting to acknowledge that her mother started off as the other woman.

"You are right, my dear, and right now, I'm having fun taking back what's mine. True love never dies, you know?"

"Love?"

"Despite what everyone would like to believe, I never stopped loving Joseph, and I know for a fact that he never stopped loving me. Your mother will just have to understand…just like I was expected to."

"You're a bitch!" Gabrielle said as she felt tears well up in the corner of her eyes, "Don't you ever compare yourself to my mom. You could never be like her, not even on her worst day."

"The compliments aren't needed, dear. I tried to tell Isabelle back then that Joseph belonged to me, but she was set on proving me wrong. Their whole marriage was a joke that went on for too long, but at least, she got you out of it, right? I always try to see the good in every situation even the *tragic* ones."

Not knowing what else to say, Gabrielle turned around to leave. She refused to give Laura the satisfaction of seeing a single tear fall from her eyes. If everything Laura said was true, she would never forgive her father. She wanted to give him the benefit of the doubt, but Laura was quite convincing.

After all these years, why now? she thought to herself as she made her way back to her car. She knew that K-2 wanted her to try and work things out with Joe before she went to her mom, but at this point, she couldn't keep her mother in the dark anymore. No matter the consequences, Isabella had the right to know, and Gabrielle was going to ensure that she got nothing but the truth.

Chapter Eight

When Jewel pulled up in front of Diamond and Hassan's house, he saw that Sacario had already beat him there. As soon as Jewel got word, he called Sacario and let him know what happened. Even though he didn't have all the details, it didn't matter. Sacario did 100 mph all the way up to Sac.

Quickly getting out of his car, Jewel ran up to the front door and incessantly rang the bell.

Ding. Dong. Ding. Dong. Ding. Dong. Ding. Dong. Ding. Dong.

"Who is it?" Diamond yelled. Her nerves were already on edge.

"Jewel…"

Knowing that he wouldn't be too far behind Sacario, she took a deep breath and opened the door. "What the fuck you ringing the doorbell like that for?"

"My bad…"

"They're in there," she sighed, pointing towards the den as she made her way back upstairs. As much as she wanted to cuss, scream, and blame Jewel for Hassan almost losing his life, she knew she couldn't. She knew the type of life they both led. It used to scare her every day not knowing whether Jewel was going to make it home or not, and now, she found herself in the same situation with Hassan. No matter how much it hurt her to know that he put his life on the line every day for something so frivolous in her eyes, she loved him and couldn't do anything other than be by his side.

Jewel opened the doors to the den to see Sacario and Hassan sitting on the couch talking. Because Hassan had his back to him, Jewel didn't see the bloody bandages that wrapped around his arm and chest.

"I'm sorry, Jewel," he said trying to stand up, but Jewel quickly insisted that he sit down as he put his hand over his shoulder.

"For what, bruh?"

"Smackz," he said putting his head down, "We were outnumbered…the shit happened so fast. I-I-I…"

"What's up, blood?" Jewel asked giving Sacario a quick dap as he sat down beside him, "Start from the beginning."

Trying to gather his thoughts before he spoke, Hassan remained silent for a few seconds.

"Tusan picked me up from the house, and we instantly slid over to the warehouse in the West. I already talked to Smackz yesterday, so I got the little passcode and whatnot. I thought we were good to go. We get there, everything seemed straight; nothing seemed out of the ordinary. We got upstairs no problem. When we finally got into the lab, I introduced Smackz and Tusan, and we were chopping it up for maybe like five or ten minutes before we suddenly heard gunshots going off outside. Smackz checked the monitors, and we saw like ten to twelve niggas masked up, dressed in all-black laying out the niggas who were supposed to be securing the building. How they knew they were even there is beyond me. I guess one of them must've gotten the keys off one of the guards 'cause before we knew it, like five of them mothafuckas ran up in the lab and started spraying. Everyone got hit except me, Smackz, and Tusan…"

"So how did he…you know?" Jewel asked, trying to swallow the knot in his throat.

"He went to the back room and grabbed his piece. When he came out, he didn't see one of the niggas coming up behind him. Before I knew it, the dude let one off in the back of his head, and it was lights out. I tried to bust back, but before I could, I got clipped in the shoulder. I remember Tusan going after them niggas too, but his gun jammed. I don't remember too much after that. I know they took off with hella work though and most of the cash that was in that mothafucka."

"All that shit is replaceable," Jewel said hanging his head.

"When I woke up, I woke up here, and Diamond had all her nurse shit spread out in the kitchen and was pulling bullets out my shoulder. My shit looked like it got ate up. Luckily, it wasn't shredded."

"You good though?"

"I'm cool…D's been feeding me pain pills all day. I'm just tryna figure out who did this shit though, bruh," Hassan said through his teeth, "I mean, first you get popped at and now Smackz. It's more than apparent that somebody is watching us and watching us closely. It makes no sense at all that somebody could get past the guards around the warehouse, let alone make it all the way into the lab. Smackz didn't deserve to go out like that, blood."

"So you niggas are really 'bout to sit here and act like you don't know who did this shit?" Sacario asked getting frustrated with the conversation. It was like everyone had their blinders on but him.

"What you mean?" Jewel asked.

"J, you don't think that it's weird as fuck that right after you and Gabrielle get shot at, one of Kisino's best soldiers shows up at the office, and then the very next day, we get hit up again?"

"Who Dash?" he asked in complete disbelief.

"Who else, blood?"

"Naw, I couldn't see that. Dash is just a kid. Whoever did this shit been in the game a long time, and they had to be watching our every move to be able to pull some shit like this off. Even if that bitch-ass nigga Kisino was still alive, he couldn't orchestrate nothing like this."

"Well, it's a big-ass coincidence then, huh?"

"Sacario, don't get me wrong, when he showed up at the office yesterday, I was feeling just like you, but after talking to him, I just didn't get that vibe. I hate to say it, but the nigga seemed sincere."

"Man…here we go," Sacario said shaking his head.

"What?"

"This is Pop all over again."

"How you figure that?"

"When Pop found out about Brandon and didn't tell you, you pushed that to the side and kept rockin' with the nigga. Even after he switched sides and literally started working for the enemy, you looked past that shit too. As much as I wanted to believe that Pop learned his lesson, I don't think he really did. He put himself in that situation to get smoked," Sacario said simply.

"We fucking put him in there," Jewel yelled, "If I never would've involved him, he would still be alive right now."

"Maybe…but he was gon' have to answer for the shit he did one day. You can't save everybody, Jewel. Betrayal never goes unanswered. You know that," he said looking him in the eyes, "And now it seems like you're doing the same shit with this nigga Dash, but the sick shit about this is that you don't even know him other than the fact that you let off a couple rounds in him and his homies. Tell me what loyalty could you possibly have to a nigga who killed two of your potnahs and left you for dead? The nigga was looking for a come-up, and he got that…at the expense of your fucking cousin, bro. I can't do this shit with you Jewel in all seriousness, not again, blood."

"Do what again?"

"You can't always be the good guy. Eventually, you gon' have to make a decision one way or another, and for the sake of every-mothafucking-body around you, it better be the right one."

$$$$$

Reagan walked into the house to see that Jewel wasn't there, but after hearing about what happened to Hassan and Smackz, she wasn't surprised. The silence in the house only echoed the loneliness she felt inside. Making sure to lock the door behind her, she made her way upstairs to lay Chase down who was asleep on her shoulder. After tucking him in safe and sound, she walked into the room she shared with Jewel and slowly sat down on the bed as she slipped her shoes off. Looking over at her side of the bed, it looked so cold. She hadn't been home in over a week, but the distance between them had been separating them long before that. She loved Jewel with everything she had, but she felt like he was slipping through her fingers, and she didn't know how to stop it.

Knowing that Jewel was preoccupied, she decided not to call him. She wanted to wait until he got home, so they could talk face-to-face. Wanting to wash the feeling of isolation off of her body, she walked into the bathroom and turned on the shower, letting the steam fill the room. As she stepped inside, she let the hot water run off her chocolate skin. For just a little while, she didn't want to think about her problems with Jewel. She just wanted to forget. For almost thirty minutes, she barricaded herself in the bathroom as Chase slept. As happy as she was to be back home, she still felt like a stranger. Something had to give.

Stepping out of the shower, Reagan slid on her robe and decided to get dinner ready for her and Chase. Even though it was late, she knew he was going to be hungry once he woke up. As she walked into the kitchen, she was surprised to see the stranger sitting at the table on his phone.

"Mi call yuh back," Tusan said quickly ending the call.

"Who the fuck are you?" Reagan asked, tightening her robe as she looked around for anything she could pick up. Spotting a butcher's knife on the counter within reach, she waited for him to make his next move.

"Mi mean no harm. Mi woulda intraduced mi'self earlier when mi heard yuh come in, but mi thought yuh were Ms. Laurie."

"Laura?" *Here we go with this shit,* she thought to herself.

"Yuh must be Jewel's wife," he said extending his hand.

"…and you are?" she asked still waiting for a response.

"Of course…," he said shaking his head, "Mi name's Tusan. Jewel's new security detail."

"Nice to meet you, Tusan, but what are you doing in my house? Where's Jewel? Where's Laura?" she asked relaxing just a little.

"Jewel had a situation ta tek care of. He ask mi ta stay behind an' look afta his son an' Ms. Laurie."

"Jailen's here?"

"He should still be asleep upstairs."

"And Laura?"

"Yuh guess is as good as mine," he said shrugging his shoulders.

$$$$$

Laura sat in the back of her town car primping herself in her compact as she waited for Joe to arrive. It had been months since they first started hooking up again. Once they saw each other in Barbados, it was like their spark had been relit. Laura did her best to resist, but soon, the familiar became inviting. She hated the idea of being the other woman, but Joe made it almost impossible to say no.

Tick. Tick. Tick. Tick.

"It's Mr. Sanchez, miss," Edward, her driver, announced.

"Let him in," she said smacking her lips together, making sure she looked like nothing but pure perfection before she slipped her mirror back into her clutch.

"Laura, it's almost midnight," Joe said climbing inside as he gave her a kiss on the cheek. Her Chanel No. 5 perfume intoxicated him. "Why couldn't this wait until morning?"

"Joseph, we need to talk," she said softly grabbing his hand.

"Well, I figured that's why I was here."

"Gabrielle stopped by tonight," she admitted. She was tired of the lies they held between them. It was time to get everything out in the open.

"What?" he asked scooting to the edge of his seat.

"Jewel had a little situation to deal with tonight. When she showed up, he thought that she was there to see him, but it was obvious that she was there to see me."

"What did she say?" he questioned. He had been trying to get in contact with Gabrielle for over a week but to no avail. All he got was her voicemail.

"What do you think she said?" Laura asked rolling her eyes, "She wanted to know what was going on with me and you."

"So…what did you tell her?"

"The truth," she said looking Joe in the eyes before he laid his head in his hands, "What, you expected me to lie forever?"

"No…well, yes…I don't know," he said shaking his head, "This is all so complicated."

"You made it that way," Laura yelled as she felt tears well up in her eyes. After almost twenty years, their divorce still hurt her. No matter what they were going through, she never stopped loving him. "What do you want, Joseph?"

"What?" he asked finally looking up at her.

"What do you want?"

As much as he wanted to say her, it wasn't that easy. He had built a life, built a family over the time they had been apart, and he didn't know if he could just let it all go.

"I know that it's selfish of me to try and keep you in this situation knowing that Isabella and I are still married."

"It is, Joseph," she said sitting back, "Do I look like the type of woman who has to creep around in the shadows like a goddamn animal? I think not! So I'm going to make this easy for you."

"How?"

"Do you love me?"

"Yes, of course, you know I do. I've loved you ever since I was a boy who barely spoke any English."

"Do you want to be with me?"

"Yes."

"Are you willing to make right what you made wrong oh so long ago?" Just as the question left her lips, his phone started to ring. It was Isabella. "…Joe? Joe? Did you hear what I just asked you?"

"Ummmmm…yeah."

"Well, are you?"

Silence continued to separate them as he stared down at his phone. He didn't know if it was a sign from God telling him to go and be with

Laura or stay with Isabella, but he knew he was going to have to choose one way or the other…and soon.

"I know that's her, Joseph," Laura said folding her arms across her chest.

"How'd you know?"

"Because I just got my answer. Good night, Joseph," she said before rolling down the window that separated her and her driver, "Edward, drop Mr. Sanchez back off at his car please."

Chapter Nine

"You can't always be the good guy. Eventually, you gon' have to make a decision one way or another, and for the sake of every-mothafucking-body around you, it better be the right one," Sacario said.

"Trust me, okay?" Jewel said looking at him in the eye. As much as he wanted to be mad, he knew he couldn't deny Sacario's concerns. In the past, his trusting ways always seemed to get him in trouble, but not this time. "Ay, I got some shit to take care of before I head back to the house. You cool, Sani?"

"Yeah, blood, it's good. I'll tap in with you tomorrow."

"Naw, you get some rest. Me and Sacario got it. Right, bruh?"

"Yeah," he said getting up to give Jewel dap. He knew that Jewel was feeling some type of way, but it needed to be said. Hassan and Jewel were like brothers to him, and he had to do what he had to do to keep them safe even if that meant pissing off Jewel in the process.

"Tell Diamond that I'll keep Jailen for the rest of the week. My mom's still out here, so it's good."

"Yep," Hassan said struggling to stand up as they briefly embraced each other before Jewel headed for the door.

As Jewel walked outside, he quickly pulled out his phone. He was tired of everyone doubting his ability to lead. Despite all of his mistakes in the past, he was done making the same ones over and over again and putting his family in danger. One thing he had learned from Golden was how to use his disadvantages as his advantages. It was time to remember all that his uncle had instilled in him.

"This is Dash. Who's this?"

"What's up, blood? This is Jewel," he said getting into his car.

"I knew you would come to your senses sooner or later, big bruh," Dash said with excitement in his voice, "So what's the plan, boss?"

"Slow your roll, bruh. There are a few things we need to figure out first."

"Shoot…"

"I don't really do too much talking over the phone, but meet me down at the office tomorrow around 10 a.m., and we'll go over all the details then."

"I'll be there at 9:30 a.m.…you won't regret this, Jewel. I promise," he said before hanging up.

Jewel knew that something was off about Dash just popping up after all this time, and he planned on figuring out what his motives really were. With Smackz gone and Hassan getting hit, there was no more room for error.

Before deciding to head home, Jewel had one more stop to make. After coming back from the Dominican Republic, things between him and Khailiah had been tense. Despite her call informing him that she wouldn't be coming to work for a while, he hadn't seen or heard from her, but he wanted to fix it. He knew what it felt like to be rejected and tossed aside by someone you have feelings for, and that was the last thing he wanted to do to her. Even though he and Reagan had a lot to work through, he cherished his friendship with Khailiah and was determined to make things right again.

Before he pulled up to her condo, he tried calling, but she sent him straight to voicemail.

"The subscriber you have reached is not available. Please leave your message after the beep…*BEEP*."

"What's up, K? It's Jewel…," he said before rolling past her car. Seeing that all the lights were on inside her place, he hung up the phone. He figured it would be better to talk in-person anyway.

Quickly parking behind her Mercedes, he jumped out, smoothed out his Dolce & Gabbana jeans, and walked up to the front door. It was going on 2 a.m., but he knew that if he didn't say what he needed to say, he may never get the chance again.

Knock. Knock. Knock. Knock.

He stood still underneath the moonlight as he waited for Khailiah to answer. After a few minutes, she finally came to the door.

"Jewel?" she asked as she slowly opened the door, revealing the all-black, lace teddy she wore, "What are you doing here? Is everything okay?" Throughout the time they had been working together, he had never been to her place. She just knew that something had to be wrong.

"Yeah, yeah, everything's fine. I just needed to holla at you for a minute."

"About?" she asked, folding her arms across her chest.

"Can I come in?" he laughed, "You acting like a nigga's a creep or something."

"...I don't know, J. It's late, and I'm not really dressed...as you can see," she said showing off her exposed flesh, "Why don't you just give me a call later?" Before he could respond, she tried to close the door hoping to end the uninvited conversation, but before she could, Jewel stuck his foot in.

"Listen, I know I'm probably the last person you wanted to see tonight, but I think we really need to talk. Just five minutes...please?"

Knowing that she wasn't going to get any sleep until she agreed, she finally gave in.

"Come in, Jewel," she said opening the door.

"You acting like you got a nigga up in here or something."

"...nope, just me," she laughed nervously, "What's up though?"

"Can we sit down?"

"Jewel, you're asking for a whole lot," she said beginning to get irritated.

"What's all the attitude for?"

"It's almost two o'clock in the morning, nigga," she snapped.

"My bad," he said as he led himself into the living room.

"Jewel, we can..."

"What's all this?" he asked cutting her off once he noticed the stacks and stacks of hundreds that sat on top of her coffee table.

"I don't really believe in banks," she said sweeping her hair out of her face.

"That gotta be like over a hundred racks though," he said sitting down on the couch, "Why you got it all out like this?"

"Inventory...so what's up, Jewel? You came over here for a reason, right?"

"...yeah, I did," he said trying to regain focus, "We need to talk."

"I get that, J, but about what though? If this is about me coming back to work, I told you that I'll let you know."

"Naw, I get that you need your little space or whatever. I just came over here to tell you that Hassan and Smackz got hit up at one of the warehouses earlier today."

"Oh, my god, are they okay?" she asked covering her mouth.

"Hassan was shot in the shoulder. He should be back at it within a few weeks, but Smackz…Smackz didn't make it."

"Jewel, I'm so sorry," she said sitting down next to him wrapping her arms around his neck as she pulled him into her, "Are you okay?"

"Yeah, I'm good, but I gotta find out who the niggas are behind this shit. First, it was me, then it's Hassan and Smackz. There's no denying that we're being targeted. I just don't understand why."

"And ya'll don't have any leads?"

"Sacario thinks that it's this young dude named Dash. He used to run with Kisino and all his people, but now, with Kisino out of the picture, him and his niggas are looking for a home."

"With the M.A.C. Boys?"

"Yeah, I guess," Jewel said putting his head down.

"Do you think that that's the best idea though? I mean, do you think that you can trust him?"

"I honestly don't know. I scheduled some time to meet with him tomorrow. I gotta feel him out some more. You know Sacario is ready to instantly write the nigga off, but I think he can be useful for the time being."

"Jewel, you're a smart dude. I know that you'll figure all this out…before it's too late," she said hugging him again.

"That's what I came to talk to you about. These niggas could be anywhere, so I just need you to keep your eyes open. If anything happened to you, I could only blame myself."

"I'm a big girl, Jewel. I know that I look all soft and pretty," she smiled as she traced her crystal-covered nail across his chest, "but I ain't new to this."

"Is that right?" he laughed.

Feeling challenged, Khailiah got up and walked into her bedroom. It didn't take long before she came out holding a .45.

"If a nigga starts bustin at me, he better be prepared for that clap back," she said aiming it right at Jewel's head.

He sat back and admired her beauty. In that moment, he couldn't deny that she looked sexy as fuck. The black gun against the all-black lace she wore was too much for him to handle.

"Girl, if you don't sit your ass down."

"I'm being serious," she said laying the gun down on the table, "I appreciate your concern, Jewel, but I promise I can take care of myself."

"I believe you, kid," he said patting the seat next him, waiting for her to come and sit back down, "I don't doubt you can. I just want to believe that I provide some value, you know?"

"Oh, you do, Jewel. You definitely do…to your wife. Remember her?"

"You let me worry about that, okay?" he sighed.

"Shit still going left with ya'll?" she asked, finally sitting down.

"I don't even know how to explain it. Every time I get ready to talk to her, she dips. I haven't seen her since before we left for D.R.," he admitted.

"What's the problem though?"

"We're just not on the same page. I mean, it's hard to be with a mothafucka who can't even stand to be in your presence for more than five minutes. As we speak, my mom is at home with Jailen, and Reagan took Chase to fucking Sacario's house."

"Do you think that with everything going on, it's smart to have them home alone like that?"

"It's good. I just hired a new security team, so they're watching the house as we speak. I dare a mothafucka to try and take it there. That would be the last bad decision they ever made."

"Security?" Khailiah asked screwing her face up.

"Yeah, after the shooting down at the office, my mom got hella 'noided, so she brought this nigga named Tusan and his boys down from Barbados."

"Tusan?"

"Yeah, I don't really know too much about him yet, but so far so good. He was there when Hassan and Smackz got hit, and from what I heard, Hassan would be bagged up somewhere too if it wasn't for Tusan."

"Do you think that it's smart to leave your mother and son with a nigga you just met?"

"That's what I pay him for."

"Sometimes money isn't enough, Jewel…just please be careful, okay?"

"Why you say all that? You act like you know the nigga or something."

"…no, nothing like that. I'm just saying, in the year I've been working for you, you never needed security before. I just want you to be careful…that's all. I don't know what I would do if anything happened to you," Khailiah said leaning back on the couch.

"I'm good…everything's gonna be good. Mark my words."

Before either of them knew it, they had been talking for hours until they couldn't escape sleep any longer. When Jewel opened his eyes, the sun was up and Khailiah was sleeping peacefully against his chest. Knowing he had to link up with Dash a little later that morning, he decided to finally go home.

"K…K…," he whispered. She stirred in her sleep at the sound of his voice. "Khailiah."

"Yeah," she said lifting her head, seeing that it was already morning.

"I'm 'bout to head to the house," he said standing up, "Thanks for letting me crash here…and vent."

"I knew you missed me," she smiled.

"I'm not even gonna front. I kinda did. I had nobody to get on my nerves all damn day."

"Yeah, okay," she laughed, "I know work isn't be the same."

"Speaking of work…"

"Jewel, I told you that I needed some…"

"I know what you said, but I need you, K.K. Just say you'll think about it."

Knowing that Jewel wasn't going to let up, she had no other choice but to say, "…okay, I'll think about it."

"I knew you wouldn't be able to stay away," he said kissing her on the cheek before he headed out of the front door.

$$$$$

When Jewel arrived home, he was surprised to see Reagan's car parked in the driveway. Preparing himself for battle, he walked into the house to see that, thankfully, everyone was still asleep. As he walked up the stairs and went into his room, Reagan was still asleep with Chase nestled underneath her side. Trying his best to be quiet, he slowly removed his clothes, hoping that he could get a few hours of sleep before he had to be down at the office.

"So you're gonna just act like you haven't been out all night?" she asked as she rolled over to face Jewel.

"Chase is sleep, Rea. We can talk about this later," he said continuing to change his clothes.

"No, fuck that! You always wanna say that I'm the one avoiding you, so we're gonna talk about this now. Where have you been?"

"If you would have been here, you would have known that Smackz was murdered yesterday and Hassan was shot. I was checking on my nigga."

"Yeah, I know all that. I called Diamond to check on you since you didn't feel like letting your wife know that your cousin had just been killed."

"Oh, so you're my wife now?" he laughed.

"Don't fucking play with me. I loved Smackz too, Jewel."

"Please don't act like you give a fuck. You've been gone for weeks. Every chance you get, you dip, taking my fucking son with you, but now you're so concerned with what's going on here? Miss me with that shit, Rea."

"How could I not be, Jewel? You got random niggas all up and through this mothafucka and don't even feel the need to tell me shit."

"Again, if you were here, you would know exactly what was going on. Why do you feel like I have to fucking report to you? You don't want to be here. You've been made that shit clear."

"Jewel, I know that you're upset right now, but don't try to blame all this on me. We're in this situation because of you."

"How you figure that?" he smirked.

"If you wouldn't have been playing house with your side-bitch this whole time, I would've had no reason to leave," she said smacking her lips.

"Here you go with this shit," he said rolling his eyes, "Please tell me how Khailiah is the source of all of our problems?"

"The fact that you don't see that she is already lets me know what time it is."

"It should let you know that you're fucking delusional. K had nothing to do with why you've been going out of your way to be a bitch!"

"Bitch?" she asked sitting up.

"Did I stutter? It's apparent that you want out of this relationship, Reagan, but this time, I'm not about to stand in your way anymore. I've gone over and beyond what a normal nigga would've put up with. I've been to fucking hell and back just to be with you to prove that I love you more than life itself, to prove that I wanted nothing more than to be with you, but I'm done with that shit. You're fucking insecure, and you're willing to let any bitch shake up what we have. I've never fucked Khailiah, and I never planned to because I'm dedicated to you and to this marriage, but if you don't believe that, Rea, fuck you," he said storming out of the room.

"Jewel, I…"

"Drop it," he yelled as he closed the door to Jailen's room behind him.

Chapter Ten

The Next Day…

"Jewel, if mi gonna be any benefit ta yuh, brudda, yuh have ta leh mi know wuh's going pun, ya know?"

"My bad, Tusan," he said as they walked into his office, "I didn't mean no disrespect. I know you're here to help and all, but with my cousin gone and my boy getting shot, I just felt like it was a personal matter that I needed to handle…on my own."

"I respec' dah," he said, sitting down once they got inside.

"Listen, I know that my mama vouched for you and everything, but this shit is still all new to me. I know from the outside looking in, it may seem like I have a silver spoon in my mouth, but I'm a street nigga. That's all I know how to be. I may have been blessed with a few more opportunities than a lot of mothafuckas, but trust and believe that everything I have, I got on my own. I'm not used to asking people for shit, feel me?"

"Yuh jes leh mi know wuh yuh need. Mi not tryna get in de way. Mi an' mi team were hire ta do a job, an' dah's wuh mi plan ta do, but mi no wan' ta step pun yuh toes in de process."

"I'm glad to hear that," Jewel smiled, "but I actually need you to make a run with me."

"Now yuh talkin' mi language, brudda," Tusan said all ears. Jewel was very hard to get close to, but Tusan finally felt like he was making some progress.

"I have a couple of meetings this week with a few distributors in LA, and I want you to come with me."

"Like backup?"

"Naw, nothing like that. I've met with these niggas before. I'm just closing the deal."

"Okay, dah sounds easy enough."

"Usually, Sacario or Hassan comes with me, but…"

"But?"

"But this time I'm taking Dash," Jewel said with certainty.

"The dude from las' time?"

"Yeah."

"Yuh sure dah's a good idea?"

"Sacario thinks that Dash and his team were behind the hit at the warehouse."

"Oh, forreal? Wuh do yuh think?"

"I just don't see it," Jewel said being honest, "I've been around a lot of thug mothafuckas in my day. Niggas that would kill ya own mother right in front of you. Whoever ran up on Smackz knew exactly what they were doing and what they were looking for, and I don't see that type of work coming from a 22-23 year old dude."

"Yuh be surprise, Jewel. Niggas can be ruthless at any age."

"Yeah, you're right. That's all the more reason why I need to figure this shit out. Dash seems like a respectable dude, but I can't even lie, I've been wrong in the past. I can't afford to be wrong again. I've already lost my cousin, and now, my uncle is looking at me like I'm in over my head. I can't lose this shit, bruh."

"Yuh should neva trust anybody 'specially in dis business," Tusan said out loud, "Everyone has a motive."

"And I plan on finding out exactly what Dash's is. That's why I'm having him meet me here today. He should be here in a few minutes," Jewel said looking down at his watch.

"Yuh wan' mi ta go?" he asked, standing up.

"Naw, stay. I want you to feel him out for me. It's always better to get another person's opinion, feel me?"

"No problem. If he up ta someting, mi be able ta smell dah shit a mile away."

"That's what I like to hear," Jewel said getting up to give him dap, "And I wanted to say thank you for holding shit down for me yesterday. I know it was a lot for me to throw on you like that, but at that moment, I felt like a nigga didn't know right from left. My head was all fucked up."

"No apologies needed, brudda. Like mi say befo', Ms. Laurie has done so much fuh mi family. Mi don' tink mi can eva repay her, so watchin' afta yuh family was de leas' mi could do."

"Well, thank you again."

"Plus, everyting was coo' 'til yuh wife try ta pull a knife pun mi," he laughed.

"Who Reagan?"

"Mi no get her name. Afta she got dere, mi figure she had everyting handle, so mi lef'."

"Man…," Jewel said shaking his head.

"Yuh have a very beautiful family, Jewel. Mek sure yuh cherish dah. Yuh neva know how easy it is ta lose dem 'til you do."

"…Mr. Sanchez," Shaunda's voice boomed through the intercom, "A 'Dashan Phillips' is here to see you."

"Send him in," he said standing up, ready to meet his little protégé in the making, "What's up, Dash?" Jewel opened the door before he could even knock. "Thanks for meeting with me."

"Of course…I'm glad you decided to hit a nigga up. I mean, after how our last meeting went, I just knew you and your boys weren't fuckin' with us."

"I just had to sort some stuff out."

"I can dig it," Dash said, taking a seat beside Tusan.

"My bad, this is my associate Tusan Cole. Tusan, this was the brotha I was telling you about."

"All good I hope," he smiled.

"We'll see," Tusan said sitting back a little.

"…so what's up?" Dash asked trying to get a feel for the vibe in the room.

"When you showed up here the other day, there was some speculation on what you and your team really wanted."

"I can understand that, but, remember, Jewel, you shot me, and three of my boys died behind the M.A.C. Boys. If this was some kind of ambush, this would be a stupid-ass way to go about it, feel me?"

"My thoughts exactly, which is why I wanna see how I can leverage you."

"However you need me, bruh bruh. Me and my niggas are ready."

"Good, 'cause we had a little situation happen that we're tryna bounce back from now."

"Situation?"

"One of our warehouses got hit. The niggas who did it took a couple hundred thousand dollars in cash, at least that much in work, and they popped my cousin."

"Damn…," Dash said putting his head down, "I'm sorry to hear that."

"It was a minor setback. The money and the product can always be replaced, but we're on the niggas' heads who killed my cousin."

"As you should be," he said looking Jewel in the eye, "You need me and my niggas to put in work or someting? We got that heat all day."

"Naw, we got that handled on this end, but thank you. With this loss, we gotta make up the dough somewhere, feel me? And that's where you come in."

"That's the opportunity we've been looking for to be a hunned with you."

"But I want to show you the ropes a little first."

"What did you have in mind?"

"The M.A.C. Boys is a very complex organization. We have our guys play positions from the very basic street-level all the way up to the executive suite," Jewel said showcasing his office, "I think you have more potential than just being a corner boy."

"…I don't know about all that, Jewel," Dash said scratching the back of his head, "I ain't really tryna be stuck in a suit and office all day…no offense."

"None taken, bruh. I know how this shit looks from the outside, but I just want you to see how you really could be rockin'."

"…what do I gotta do?" he asked a little hesitant to Jewel's request.

"I got a few meetings in LA this week, and I want you to fly out there with me."

"Why me though?"

"Listen, to have been a high-ranking nigga in Kisino's camp, I know you have to be on your shit. The nigga was crazy as fuck, but he wasn't stupid, so I know that you could bring more value to the organization than you may want to admit right now. And the fact that you had balls enough to show your face after I almost took your head off shows me that you're serious about this shit. I mean, what's stopping me from finishing the job right here, right now?" Jewel laughed as he looked back and forth between Dash and Tusan.

"…nothing, I guess," Dash said fidgeting in his seat a little.

"Exactly…my niggas are ready as we speak to finish what I started if need be, but I see more in you, and I know you're smarter than that. Playing with the M.A.C. Boys is like literally playing with your life, and you don't come across as a stupid mothafucka to me."

"Never that," he said poking out his chest.

"Go on this run with me and see how we really fuck with it, and if it's not something that you're into, you can walk away from this shit, no questions asked."

"No questions asked?"

"It'll be like it never happened," Jewel assured him.

"Alright…I'm down," Dash hesitated to say.

"You scared?" he smiled.

"Naw…I'm good, blood."

"I'll be in touch in the next few days with more details."

"Sounds good," Dash said getting up before he walked out of the room.

Jewel waited until the door closed before he spoke. "So what you think?" he asked, facing Tusan.

"De young boy's scared, Jewel. Yuh really tink dah he is ready fuh all dis?"

"Of course he's not, but that's not the point. The whole reason for him coming on this trip is to find out what he really knows, and the only way I'ma be able to get to the truth is by making him trust me. Every nigga wants to feel like you're willing to put more in their hands…that you're willing to invest in them."

"But wuh if he try ta use dis shit against yuh?"

"I guess we're just gonna have to wait and see then, huh?"

"Jewel?" Khailiah said walking into his office, "…oh, I'm sorry. I didn't know you were meeting with a client. I probably should've checked in with Shaunda first."

"Naw, it's good. This is Tusan Cole, the new Head of Security."

"Nice to meet you," she said walking up and extending her hand, "I'm Khailiah Moore."

"Nice ta meet yuh," he smiled.

"Uhhh, Jewel, I came to talk to you about me coming back to work, but I can just come back later or something."

"I just got out of a meeting, so I got time," he said standing up, happy that she had finally taken his words to heart, "Tusan, blood, can you give us a few minutes?"

"Yeah, of course. Mi need ta meet up wit' some of mi men 'specially wit' dis trip comin' up. Mi gon' need all hands pun deck."

"I don't think you'll need the whole squad for lil' 'ol Dash, but do what you gotta do."

"Mi be in touch," Tusan said before he walked out of the office.

"So are you really ready to come back?"

"Yeah," she admitted, "I see you can't run this shit without me, so I figured I might as well do you a favor, you know?"

"Well, thank you, Khailiah. Things haven't been the same without you."

"Oh, I know," she said sitting down, crossing her thick thighs as her pencil skirt began to inch up.

"But things can't be how they were before."

"Here we go," she said rolling her eyes, "Jewel, I thought we got past all that. I admit that you caught me in a moment of weakness, but I promise it will never…"

"No, not 'cause of that…but because I can't have you in the middle of the crossfire. Smackz is dead, and Hassan almost met his maker too. Shit is too risky right now for me, for the whole clique, but especially for you."

"Jewel, I appreciate all your concern, but you are not my nigga."

"Excuse me?"

"Listen, you said that we can't be together because you're married, and I have no other choice but to respect that. As much as I wish that wasn't the case, that's the reality of the situation. You gotta let this shit be. Either I'm 100% a part of the team or I'm not, but I don't need you protecting me like I'm some little-ass girl who's incapable of doing her job. I knew what I was signing up for. Golden made it more than clear that this shit was literally a matter of life and death, and I still chose to stay. I know that you're just tryna look out for me, but I'm not Reagan. I can handle my own."

$$$$$

Reagan tossed and turned all morning thinking about the fight she had with Jewel. Tired of fighting 24/7, she was ready to throw in the towel, but she knew she couldn't. She loved Jewel and had gone over and beyond to ensure that they stayed together even when he had moved on in the past. She couldn't give up that easily. She couldn't stop fighting for him, for their marriage no matter how hard it was. She had to think about her family, the family they were raising together. The boys deserved more from the both of them.

After Jewel left for work, Reagan went downstairs to the guestroom to see if Laura could watch the kids for her for a few hours. Laura got in a little before Jewel did, so Reagan knew she was probably exhausted, but it was an emergency. Without too much begging, Laura agreed. She was willing to do anything to take her mind off Joe…at least for a little while.

Wanting to show Jewel that she was still all in, she threw on her sexiest outfit, did her hair and makeup, and slipped on a pair of strappy turquoise Gucci sandals before she headed out the door. She was on a mission. After spending forty-five minutes in Sacramento's mid-morning traffic, she stopped and grabbed a venti *Chai Crème Frappuccino* from Starbucks. It had been a while since she had seen the world in the morning. Her depression kept her so isolated that she usually hid from the sunlight.

Making sure she had everything in order, Reagan parked her red Lexus RX in the parking lot across the street from Jewel's office.

"You can do this, Reagan," she said to herself as she tried to exhale her anxiety, "Jewel loves you, and nothing or no one can take that away. You know that." Checking her face in the overhead mirror to make sure it was still flawless, she applied another coat of M.A.C.'s *Viva Glam Ariana II* before she stepped out of her car and made her way down towards the building. Even though she was nervous, she knew there was no turning back. If Jewel wanted her to fight for him, fight for their marriage, then that's exactly what she planned to do.

"What's up, Shaunda?" she smiled as she walked inside.

"Hey, Reagan, girl," Shaunda said getting up to give her a hug, "Where have you been?! I feel like I haven't seen you in months."

"I know. I've just been so busy with the gym and Chase…and everything."

"Girl, don't I know it," she laughed, "This shit don't stop. We gotta be Superwoman out here."

"Who you telling?"

"I know you came up here looking for ya man coming in here looking like that."

"Yeah, I thought I would come and take him out for a late breakfast."

"Well, you're just in luck. He had a meeting maybe fifteen-twenty minutes ago, but he just wrapped up, and his schedule is clear for the rest of the morning," she winked.

"Perfect!" Reagan smiled.

"You want me to call up and let him know you're on your way?"

"No, that's okay. I want it to be a surprise."

"I got you, girl. I swear ya'll are relationship goals. I keep praying that the universe blesses me with someone as sexy and successful as Jewel," she said playing with her high, waist-length ponytail.

Be careful what you ask for, Reagan thought to herself.

"Make sure you come down and see me before you leave," Shaunda said before she answered the phone that had been ringing ever since Reagan arrived, "*Sanchez & Associates,* this is Shaunda. How may I direct your call?"

"I will," she said waving as she made her way to the elevator.

Compared to a few of Jewel's other secretaries, Reagan liked Shaunda the best. Even though she talked more than anybody she had ever met in her life, she was a very sweet girl and never gave her any reason to make her look at her twice, not like Khailiah. From the moment she met Khailiah, Reagan already knew her M.O. Jewel pretended to be oblivious to the fact that she was romantically interested in him, but Reagan could see right through all of her Maybelline. Khailiah wanted Reagan's spot, and she was scared that she was willing to go to any length to snatch it away from her. Blaming Reagan's suspicions on paranoia, Jewel never really took her concerns seriously. Reagan wanted to trust him. When it came to other women, he never gave her a reason not to. As much as she wanted to follow her gut, she put her insecurities aside for the sake of her marriage and trusted in her husband. If Jewel said nothing was going on, then nothing was going on.

Ding.

As the elevator doors opened, she ran right into Tusan.

"Hey, it's you again," she said stepping out as she fixed her mid-length dress.

"…Tusan. Mi name is Tusan," he smiled as he towered over her, holding a cup of coffee.

"Right…well, nice to see you again."

"Yeah, yuh too. Mi glad ta see dah dere no weapons 'round dis time."

"I wasn't gonna stab you," she laughed, "Unless you gave me a reason to."

"Well, mi really sorry dah had ta be our first impression, ya know?"

"No biggie," she said shrugging her shoulders, "I've met people a lot worse than that before. Believe me."

"Leh's do it ova."

"Huh?"

"Mi name's Tusan Cole," he said lifting her hand, letting his dreads sweep across her as he gently placed a kiss upon her skin, "It is very nice ta meet yuh, Reagan."

"Likewise," she blushed.

"So yuh here ta see Jewel?"

"Yeah, his secretary said he just got out of a meeting, so I thought that I would just pop in."

"Yuh jes miss yuh chance den," he said putting his hand in his pants pocket.

"What you mean?"

"A girl name…Khailiah stop by ta talk ta him. It seem urgent."

"Khailiah?" Reagan asked rolling her eyes. *That must be why he flew his black-ass out of the house like that this morning.*

"But bein' Jewel's wife, mi pretty sure yuh already know her."

"Oh, do I," she said smacking her lips, "Tusan, it was really nice to see you again, but let me get in here. If Khailiah is here, I definitely want to make sure that I get to say, 'hi', you know?"

"Of course," he said clearing a path for her with his hand, "Mi sure we'll get ta talk lata."

All she could do was smile as she calmly made her way to Jewel's office.

"Reagan, it's nothing. Reagan, it's nothing," she repeated to herself with each step she took. Her blood was boiling, but the last thing she wanted to do was cause a scene.

Without knocking, she opened the door to see Khailiah sitting on Jewel's desk in front of him with her shoes on the floor beneath her as they continued to talk.

"Rea?" he said as he looked towards the door.

"So this is why you ran out of the house so fucking early this morning?" she asked closing it behind her as she looked Khailiah up and down.

"Man…please don't tell me that you came all the way down here on some bullshit."

"…I'll give you guys some time to talk. Jewel, I'll be in my office if you need me. I'm pretty sure I have hundreds of messages to get through," Khailiah said as she slid off his desk, slipping her pink, freshly manicured toes back into her patent-leather Louboutin pumps.

"Oh, no, bitch, you'd probably want to stay for this," Reagan said crossing her arms over her chest.

"Excuse me?"

"Now that all three of us are here in the same room, I figured we might as well get some shit out in the open."

"Reagan, this is not the time or place for this, bruh. Please try and act like you remember where the fuck you are right now."

"Oh, I'm fully aware, Jewel, but since I can't get any answers from *you*, I might as well get them from your hoe-potnah."

"Look, I ain't gon' be too many more bitches and hoes before…"

"Before what, bitch?"

"Jewel, get your wife before they'll be escorting my ass up on out of here. I'm tryna keep shit cute…," Khailiah smirked.

"Listen, all this back and forth chit chat is for the birds," Reagan said sitting down as she turned her chair to face her, "Woman to woman, I just need to know one thing."

"And what's that?"

"Are…you…fucking…my…husband?" Reagan didn't move a muscle as she waited for her to answer. The way she was feeling she prayed she had enough sense to say the right thing.

"I know what happened in D.R. can be misconstrued as…"

"What happened in D.R.? What is she talking about?" Reagan asked looking right at Jewel.

"K.K., I didn't say anything…about what happened," he sighed.

"Oh…sorry."

"So why don't you fill me in since my so-called husband wants to keep me out of the loop?"

"Rea, we can talk about all this when we get home," Jewel pleaded.

"Naw, fuck that! So what happened between you and Jewel?" she asked returning her focus to Khailiah.

"In a moment of weakness…"

"Khailiah, we don't need to do this here…"

"Jewel, shut the fuck up and let this bitch talk! For months, I've been tryna get you to talk to me…and nothing. I'm tired of being the only one left in the dark."

"I'm really not tryna get in the middle of ya'll marriage…"

"Bitch, you've been in the middle, so you might as well just spit it out."

"…we kissed."

"What?" Reagan snapped.

"But it was 100% my fault. Jewel didn't let it go any further than that. It's a mistake that I wish I could take back, but…"

"And you expect me to believe that?" she laughed, "Bitch, you've been tryna to suck this nigga's dick ever since the first day you met him."

"I mean, I don't really care what you believe. That's the…"

Before Khailiah could finish her sentence, Reagan grabbed her by her hair with one hand and began to punch her in the face with the other. Khailiah screamed as she struggled to loosen Reagan's grip, but her efforts were useless.

"Bitch, you think it's cute to be fucking a married man?" she asked, hitting her over and over again. She had so much built-up frustration from Jewel, from the situation with Khailiah, from everything, so it felt good to finally be able to get a little release.

"Rea, stop!" Jewel said as he tried to unwrap Khailiah's hair from in between her fingers, but Reagan was determined.

"Fuck this bitch," she spat.

Hearing all of the commotion coming from inside the office, security ran in not prepared for what they saw. They looked to Jewel for some sort of direction, but he looked just as lost as they did.

"Rea!"

"Bitch, get off me," Khailiah said finally able to pull herself away from Reagan.

"Every time I see you, I'm tagging that ass," she said trying to spit on her, "You think that you could come to my house, be around my kids, be fucking my husband the whole time, and I was just gonna let that shit slide? Bitch, you found the wrong one."

"We never fucked!" Jewel and Khailiah said together, but their words fell on deaf ears.

"Ya'll might as well…get this trash up on…out of here," Reagan said out of breath as she motioned towards the security guards.

"Naw, naw," Jewel said pulling Khailiah aside as she sat down in his chair. The bruises on her face were already starting to form. "Would ya'll mind escorting my wife downstairs please?"

"Me?!" Reagan screamed, "Jewel, after all this shit, you're kicking *me* out?"

"Reagan, what the fuck do you expect? You came up here acting like an asshole. Yeah, she kissed me, but I didn't tell you for this exact reason. I knew that you would blow this shit out of proportion."

"Out of proportion? Jewel, if the roles were reversed, what would you do?"

"The roles have been reversed…remember that," he said handing Khailiah a cold bottled water as she applied it to her face, hoping to bring down the swelling.

"Fuck you!"

"Mike, Paul, please see to it that my wife makes it back to her car safely. Rea, we'll talk about this when I get home."

Without saying another word, Reagan stormed out of his office in complete disbelief as security followed closely behind her.

"I fucking got this," she said, rapidly tapping the elevator button, trying to make it come faster, "I don't need ya'll fucking following me. I know where I parked."

"We're just obeying orders, Mrs. Sanchez."

"No need. I'm leaving, okay?" she said as she stepped into the elevator hoping that they couldn't see the tears that were beginning to form in the corners of her eyes.

She felt like an eternity had passed as the elevator slowly descended and a sweet and calming melody surrounded her. She couldn't believe that once again Jewel had taken Khailiah's side over hers. She began to wonder what she was even fighting for anymore.

Ding.

"Hey, girl, that was fast…," Shaunda said as she stepped off the elevator, but Reagan just kept walking.

In a haze, she walked outside and waited for the traffic to clear. As the cars passed her, her head began to spin and everything around her disappeared.

"…Reagan? Reagan?"

"Huh?" she said once she finally heard her name.

"Yuh good? Yuh look like yuh jes seen a ghost or someting," Tusan said walking up behind her, "I tek it dah de meeting didn't go too well."

"Why you say that?" she asked still in a fog.

"Yuh bleedin'," he said gently wiping away the trickle of blood that began to form on her forehead.

"That bitch!"

"I knew someting like dis would happen," he said shaking his head.

"How could you have known?" she scoffed.

"Mi imagine dah no woman is good wit' her man stayin' de night wit' anotha woman."

"Excuse me?"

"Dah's why yuh were fightin', right? 'Cause Jewel spen' de night at Khailiah's house las' night?"

Reagan felt like the wind had been knocked out her…again. Not even bothering to respond, she pulled her phone out of her purse and texted Jewel.

I hope that bitch's bed is still warm from last night 'cause you bet not bring your black-ass home. It's over! I want a divorce.

Chapter Eleven

Joe stared up at the ceiling completely alone in his solitude. Now that the secret was out about his infidelity, he knew he couldn't hide from it anymore. Isabella had been calling and calling ever since the night he met up with Laura, but he never answered. He had no idea what to say. What started off as a brief trip down memory lane quickly turned into something so much more. He was confused. He and Laura had been through hell and had every reason to hate each other, but when he went to Barbados, it was like none of their pain had ever existed. Laura was his firsts of many, and even though he tried to deny it for so long, she still held a huge place in his heart, and it scared him. He thought that he had gotten her out of his system long before making it official with Isabella, but there she remained. Laura was like a drug to him, and he was having a hard time shaking her. It wasn't fair to his wife though; it wasn't fair to her for him to be stuck in the middle, confused about where he really wanted to be. Despite his past life with Laura, Isabella had been his life. She helped shape him into the man he was, and he would never be able to repay her for that. They had built a beautiful family together, and he knew that he owed her more than to be tucked off in a hotel somewhere. As much as he wished he could've avoided the conversation, he knew he had to face the truth. It was time.

Ring. Ring. Ring. Ring.

"Joe?" Isabella softly said into the phone.

"Yeah…Izzy, it's me."

"Oh, thank God," she sighed in relief, "When you didn't answer the phone, I didn't know what to think. I was on the verge of calling…"

"Izzy, I'm fine."

"Well, where are you? You haven't been home."

"I just needed to clear my head, but I think we need to talk."

"So what Gabby said is really true then?" she asked in disbelief.

"I really don't want to do this over the phone," Joe said putting his face in his hand, "I think that it'll be better if we sit down together and discuss a few things."

"You know where to find me," she said hanging up.

Taking a deep breath, Joe gathered up the few things he had brought with him before calling downstairs to the front desk to order more towels. He didn't know how Isabella was going to take the news, so he figured, he'd rather be safe than sorry. An hour later, he pulled up in his driveway and sat idly for a few minutes. He had only been gone for a night, but the house in front of him seemed so unfamiliar.

How did I get here? he thought to himself.

At that moment, he wished he could've talked to his father, but he knew he didn't have much time. Time was of the essence, and plus, he already knew what Joseph Sr.'s response would have been.

"Go home," he used to tell Joe, but he was stubborn back then and refused to listen. Joseph Sr. adored Laura. She was the mother to his only grandson, and she had made it her duty to see to it that the Sanchez-Smith cartel thrived even after her father's death. Laura was dedicated to their family despite all of Joe's indiscretions. Losing her family wasn't an option for her until she no longer had a choice. Letting go of Joe and Jewel was one of the hardest things she ever had to do, and she regretted it each and every day of her life. She would often run to Joseph Sr. in hopes of answers, but this time, he had none. He knew his son wanted to prove himself to the world, so he would tell her that whatever Joe was going through had to run its course. He never imagined it would've taken this long though.

Although Joe loved Isabella, being with her was really to spite his family. Since birth, he was told how to live his life, what to wear, how to act, who to be, and he was sick of it. Being with Isabella was the first decision he made on his own, and that elation guided him through their relationship. He finally felt like a man, but now, he felt like he was waking up from their dream.

Knowing that he couldn't procrastinate any longer, Joe took another deep breath and stepped out of the car. Walking up the path that led to his front door, his keys jingled as his hands shook with each step he took. Before he could put the key in the lock, the door swung open.

"I thought that was you…," Gabrielle said with a disgusted look spread across her face. Not bothering to answer, Joe continued to walk inside when he found Isabella sitting down on the couch in the living room.

"…hey," he managed to say as he sat down across from her. From her puffy eyes and the dried tear stains that lined her cheeks, he could tell that she had been crying. Even though he never intended to, once again, his selfish ways were hurting someone he loved.

"Listen, I know that things are a little confusing right now."

"Confusing?" Gabrielle snapped, "You fucking Jewel's mom is more than a little confusing, Dad. You gon' have to come better than that."

Joe knew that he hurt his daughter as well, but he would have to have a conversation with her later. Right now, he was focused on his wife. Ignoring Gabrielle once again, he continued.

"There isn't any excuse that I can give you that would make any of this make sense right now."

"I don't need any excuses from you, Joe. I just need the truth…please."

"Last year when Gabrielle had the baby, Jewel flew out to Barbados, and I went out there too."

"So you've been fucking Jewel's mom for a whole year?" Gabrielle asked in disbelief, "You lied and said that you were working. While I was laid up giving birth to your granddaughter, you were out getting your dick wet?"

"Gabrielle…please," he yelled, "This isn't fucking about you."

"Excuse me?"

"I know that you are just trying to look out for your mother because you love her, but this has nothing to do with you. This is between me and my wife, okay?"

"You mean to tell me that I catch you dickin' down Laura, and the shit has nothing to do with me? Puhlease…it has everything to do with me. Against popular belief, your actions affect everyone in this family…not just you!"

"Bye, Gabrielle," Joe said standing up and walking toward the front door.

"What? You're kicking *me* out?"

"I know that we have our own issues to sort out, but now is not the time."

"Fuck that! I'm not going nowhere," she said sitting down on the couch, crossing her legs.

"Gabby…," Isabella began.

"I'm not going to ask you again, Gabrielle. I am still your father before anything else."

"You're not shit to me, just another lying, cheating, manipulative-ass dog…"

Walking back into the living room, Joe yanked her up by her arm and dragged her towards the front door.

"Owwwwww," she screamed as she tried to pull away, but his grip only got tighter, "Let me go!"

"Like I said, I am still your father, and you're going to respect me. I don't care what your mother and I are going through. Do you understand me, Gabrielle?" he asked, slinging her outside.

"Fuck you," she spat.

"I love you too," he said closing the door in her face as she continued to yell, scream, and beat against the door.

Isabella just wanted to know what the hell was going on, so she overlooked her daughter's tantrum.

"Joe, can you please talk to me?" she asked, trying to keep her composure. From what Gabrielle told her, she was well aware of the situation. She just wanted to hear it from him.

"When I went to Barbados," he said sitting back down, "I went for the sole purpose of talking Jewel out of going to see my father. Once I found out that he had been requested, I knew that could only mean one thing."

"That you and Laura were getting back together?" she yelled.

"Of course not. It meant that my father and Laura were going to reveal Jewel's true identity to him and pull him further into the life that he already was in, and I didn't want that for my son."

"Please explain to me what Laura has to do with Jewel after all this time?"

"I went out there to save my son from the life that I knew was going to be bestowed upon him, but I was too late. He already had his mind made up. There was nothing I could do. He was set to go to D.R., and I knew that if I didn't go with him to support him, I would lose Jewel forever…"

"Joe, please just get to the fucking point," Isabella said sitting back with her arms folded across her chest, "I feel like you're just giving me the run around."

"Izzy, please just let me finish…"

"I mean, Jewel has nothing to do with you and Laura."

"But that's where you're wrong. After the trip to see my father, Jewel got ready to head back home with Reagan and the baby, but I…I stayed behind."

"Why?"

"Me and Laura had a few things to discuss."

"Like what, Joe? Like you fucking her? Huh?"

"I know how it seems, but my intentions were never to hurt you…never in a million years. I love you."

"You don't love me, Joe. You only love yourself. After all we've been through, how could you do this to me, to our family?"

"It wasn't planned. Laura and I finally got to talk about everything that happened between us, our marriage, my infidelity, the divorce…everything, and it made me realize that we were both hurt and did whatever we could to hurt each other even more. I know it was wrong for me to sleep with her, but I fell back into the familiar. I did love her at one point in time, you know?"

"And that makes it okay?" she yelled, "We have been together for over twenty years, Joe. Raquel looks at you like her father, and now you're telling me that everything we've built, all of a sudden, means absolutely nothing to you?"

"I never said that," he said putting his head down.

"You don't have to," she said dabbing her eyes as her tears began to fall again, "Get out."

"What?"

"Get out!"

Joe knew that Isabella needed time to process everything. As much as he didn't want to leave, he decided to give her her space. The conversation wasn't over by a long shot, and eventually, he knew he had a choice to make, but tonight…he just wanted to disappear into the shadows.

$$$$$

"Ay, nigga, turn that up," a guy sitting in K-2's chair said, trying to refrain from bobbing his head to the beat that filled the room as he continued to get his hair cut

"That's my lil' homie Serg," K-2 said with pride.

"From the M.A.C. Boys?"

"You know it, nigga."

Even though K-2 let go of his dope boy dreams and finally settled into reality, his affiliations never changed. It took some getting used to, but he was able to let go of the street life for his family's sake. Gabrielle and Nevaeh meant the world to him, and he was willing to do anything to ensure that they were protected even if that meant sacrificing everything he had ever known in the process. The transition from the streets to going legit wasn't as difficult as he thought it would be. *Rich City Cutz* was bringing in more money than he ever expected, and he got to do one of the things he loved. He had to admit that Gabrielle was a huge part of his success. If it wasn't for all of her work behind the scenes, he would still be cutting niggas' hair in his garage.

"I'm surprised to hear that them niggas still breathing and walking around after what happened the other day."

"What you mean?" K-2 asked as he faded up his sides. Even though Sacario tried to keep him as far away from the drama as he could for his own sake, K-2 made sure to keep his ears to the streets. No matter where he was or what he was doing, the M.A.C. Boys would always be like family.

"Man, if you ain't heard, I ain't tryna be up in here gossiping like a lil' bitch."

"Nick, blood," he said turning off the clippers as he waited for a few customers to pass by, "If you know something I need to know, you might as well tell me. I mean, I know I don't bang no more, but them still my niggas. And you know how Sacario is…so stop playing with me."

"Alright," he said turning around to face K-2 as he briefly admired his handiwork in the mirror that sat behind him, "I don't know too much, but from what I heard, the M.A.C. Boys got hit the other day and got hit hard. My nigga said like twenty niggas ran up in one of they spots and started bustin'. Everyone got popped…even Sani Bo."

"Swear, blood?" K-2 said, scratching his head as he stared down at the floor. He knew Sacario was only trying to look out for him, but he wasn't with all of the secrets that he held between them.

"I think Sani's cool, but Jewel's cousin didn't make it."

"Smackz?"

"Yep."

"So who they saying took out the hit?"

"That's the craziest part, feel me?" Nick said loosening the black nylon cape that was draped around his neck, "It's a lot of speculation. It's plenty of niggas who would want to take credit for knocking the M.A.C. Boys off, but this was some other-ass shit."

"Some out-of-town niggas?" K-2 asked as he leaned against his station.

"You know it, nigga. Some Jamaicans I think. I'm not too sure though 'cause you know how niggas like to talk, but that's what it's looking like."

Jamaicans? That don't even sound right, K-2 thought to himself. Something was up, and he planned on getting to the bottom of what exactly what it was.

After finishing up Nick's haircut and getting a few more customers out of the way, K-2 decided to close up the shop early for the day. If Sacario wasn't going to come up off of the information about what happened to Smackz and Hassan willingly, he had no other choice but to force his hand.

Tick. Tick. Tick.

K-2 hurried to unlock the door as Sacario patiently waited outside.

"Yo, what's the emergency? I came down as soon as I got your message," he said walking inside, "You cool?"

"I'm good," K-2 said sitting down in his chair after he relocked the door, "You good?"

"Yeah…why wouldn't I be?" Sacario smiled.

"Nigga, stop all this fake shit," he said through his teeth.

"What's up, blood?"

"That's what I'm tryna figure out."

"Look, say whatever you gotta say 'cause I ain't feeling all this back and forth shit, bruh."

"What happened to Smackz?"

Damn, Sacario thought. He knew K-2 was going to find out sooner or later, but he was really hoping for later.

"He got popped," he said putting his head down.

"How?"

"Does it matter? He's gone now."

"Yes, it fucking matters. You out here playing me like I'm some bitch or someting."

"How you figure that?" Sacario asked, sitting down on the red leather couch that sat right in front of K-2.

"I've seen plenty of niggas…my niggas get they shit split right in front of my face more times than I can even count. I know you just tryna look out, but you not protecting me from no shit I've never seen before, bruh."

"I never said that…"

"So what is it then?"

"You not a M.A.C. Boy anymore, my nigga, so I don't feel like I have to explain shit to you," Sacario said plainly.

"Like that?" K-2 laughed.

"All the way like that."

"Well, I hate to break it to yo' bitch-ass, but technically, neither are you. If you forgot, you, Jewel, and Hassan are fucking suppliers. You not thuggin' it on the block no more, Cari."

"I know what my job is…thank you."

"So what happened?"

Sacario was hesitant to speak. K-2 had done so much to get out of the life, and Sacario didn't want to do anything that was going to bring him back into the underworld even if that meant keeping him tucked away in the shadows.

"Cari!" K-2 yelled snapping him back from his thoughts.

"Yeah?"

"What happened? And don't try to give me no cookie cutter-ass answer either, bruh."

"Hassan went down to the warehouse in the West to link up with Smackz. Smackz had upped his shipment by a couple hundred a month, so he had hella product he had to break down. Sani really just went down there to see if he needed help with anything. Like ten minutes later, they got hit…"

"How? That mothafucka is like a fortress," K-2 said shaking his head.

"That's what we're still tryna find out now. I mean, whoever set this shit up had to have some inside information. There's no way a nigga off the street would be able to just walk up and pull that shit off. Anyway…they ran up the stairs to the lab and started taking niggas out. Sani got hit in the shoulder, so he had to fall back, but Smackz…Smackz wasn't so lucky, blood," Sacario said putting his head down, "Jewel's uncle is making funeral arrangements now."

"Damn, I really didn't want to believe that shit."

"You heard about Smackz already?"

"Nigga, you know I heard about the shit already. What you think I called you down here for?"

"Who told you?"

"Nick."

"Nick from Oak Park?"

"Yep."

"What was he doing all the way down here?"

"You know niggas come from all over to get cut by the best," K-2 said popping his collar.

"Be serious, K."

"Nigga, I am," he laughed, "Nick was getting cut when he asked about Serg's new CD I was playing, and the conversation went from there."

"What he say?"

"Basically, the same shit you did. I wish I would've heard it from you though to be honest."

"I hate to break it to you, K, but you were the last mothafucka to cross my mind…no offense."

"None taken, nigga, but the fact that I've been seeing yo' black-ass every day for the past couple of days and you haven't bothered to say shit really fucked with me, Cari, blood. I may not be in the clique officially anymore, but they will always be my niggas."

"I wasn't thinking like that…my bad."

"I know you weren't," he said shaking his head, "Well, now that I'm all caught up, whose heads we on?"

"That's the thing…we don't know. I mean, I do…but Jewel is playin' Captain Save-a once again."

"What?"

"You ain't ever gon' believe who mysteriously popped up a day before all this shit went down."

"Who?"

"Remember when me, you, and Pop went up to the *Super 8* looking for Kisino?"

"Yeah, how could I forget? You niggas did leave me in the car."

"You was lookout, K…"

"Yeah, whatever."

"Anyway, when we got to the spot where Kisino was, he had some of his men guarding the door. We knocked them off real smoove, feel me? But after that, two more of his niggas came out ready to start bustin'."

"And ya'll took them out, right?"

"Just one of them. The other one who got away, Dash, he was the nigga Jewel shot up when him and Pop went over to Valley Hi."

"Damn…"

"Right! So the day before all this goes down, Dash shows up at Jewel's office."

"And says what?"

"That he wants in."

"Wants in what?"

"Wants in the M.A.C. Boys?"

"You gotta be kidding me, blood."

"I wish I was, bruh. I couldn't make this shit up even if I tried."

"And Jewel just said it was good?"

"Basically…you know how he is, and especially since Pop died, he feels like he has to do something to make shit right again."

"So you really feel like this Dash dude was behind the hit?"

"Yep," Sacario said with certainty, "I mean, who else could it be?"

"You're wrong on this, bruh."

"What?" he asked, screwing his face up, "How would you know?"

"Nick said it was some out-of-town niggas."

"Out-of-towners?"

"Yep…Nick said it was some Jamaicans."

Sacario sat back and tried to run the scenario through his head. He just knew that Dash and his boys were behind the hit, so what K-2 was telling him didn't make any sense.

"Naw," he said shaking his head, "It has to be Dash."

"It's not, bruh. I don't know who these niggas are, but if you want to find out what happened, you gon' have to look elsewhere. Everything you told me, Nick already told me earlier. Obviously, somebody knows something."

"I gotta call Hassan."

$$$$$

Hassan lied on Diamond's stomach as she greased and massaged his scalp. Ever since he was shot, he had no choice but to stay at home with her, and she was loving it. She knew that it was only a matter of time before he was back out on the streets, so she planned to enjoy every minute she could with him.

"So when you want to get this thang poppin'?" he asked as he kissed her small baby bump, "I know you want to do this before that thang really starts poking out."

"Uh, duh…," she laughed, "I already started looking for dresses. I think I found something at Miosa. I just gotta find Jailen something to wear."

"You let me worry about that. Me and lil' man gon' be laced. Don't you even trip about that," he said sitting up and placing a kiss on her lips.

Ring. Ring. Ring. Ring. Ring.

"I thought you said you turned that thing off?" Diamond sighed.

"Babe, that's the Bat Phone. You know I gotta keep that on at all times," he said rolling over towards the nightstand. It was Sacario. "What's up with you, bruh?" he asked as Diamond rolled her eyes.

"Ain't nothing. You at the house?"

"Yep, where you at?"

"I just left K's shop."

"Oh, forreal? What that nigga up to?"

"Same 'ol same 'ol, but he had some news for me."

"Like what?"

"When you and Tusan went to the spot, did those niggas ever say anything?"

"Naw, I mean, they never said anything to me. From the looks of it, they knew exactly where they were going, so they didn't need any help, feel me?"

"Yeah, well, K said he heard they were some out-of-town niggas."

"Out-of-towners?"

"Yeah, from Jamaica or somewhere."

"What would they be doing all the way out here?"

"I guess that's what we gotta find out, but, ay, I'm on my way out there now. Me, you, and Jewel need to talk ASAP, so keep your phone on."

"Yep."

"One," Sacario said hanging up.

"Jamaica?" Hassan mumbled to himself, "What the fuck would some Jamaicans hit the M.A.C. Boys up for?" Shit wasn't sounding right to him.

"What was all that about?" Diamond asked, folding her arms across her chest.

"Not now, D," he said still deep in thought, "Not Tusan…it couldn't be."

"Hassan, I'm getting so sick and tired of this shit. How do we go from talking about our wedding to you getting wrapped up in some bullshit with Sacario?"

"Diamond, please, I really don't have time for this shit right now," he snapped.

"What the fuck is so important?"

"Somebody is tryna take out the M.AC. Boys, and the nigga could be right under our fucking noses."

"What does that have to do with you?"

"What you mean?"

"Hassan, we're building our family together. When are you gonna let all this street shit go?"

"Don't start, D. You knew this was what I did way before I even met you."

"You have your fucking college degree, Hassan. Please tell me why this is so important to you?"

"You wouldn't understand," he said slipping his sweatpants on, "I gotta call Jewel."

Chapter Twelve

The Next Day…

Jewel, Tusan, and Dash arrived at LAX as the bright sun shined down on them. Dash had never been out of Sacramento before, so the trip was much needed.

"How you feeling, bruh?" Jewel asked as he placed his hands on Dash's shoulder.

"Better now. I can't even lie…that plan ride had a nigga spooked, but that xany I popped had me floating."

"Well, good, but I'ma need you to pull it together before this meeting. We gon' go to the hotel first to chill for a second, but then we're heading straight there."

"No problem, blood. I won't fuck this up…I promise."

Ring. Ring. Ring. Ring

Jewel looked down at his phone to see that it was Hassan calling…again. He knew he needed to check in with him, but he pressed *Ignore* instead. He couldn't get Sacario's words out of his head. He knew that in the past he had jeopardized everyone around him, but this time was going to be different.

"You ready?" he asked, looking back at Tusan as their car pulled up.

"Lea' de way, brudda," Tusan said throwing their bags in the trunk.

Forty-minutes later, they pulled up in front of the Omni. Jewel was exhausted, but he still had work to do. As much as he wanted to go with his gut, he had to take into account what Sacario had to say too. He had been blind for so long when it came to people and their loyalties toward him, but with Smackz gone and Hassan injured, he had to step it up.

"Jewel, yuh ready?" Tusan asked as he held open the car door, snapping him back from his thoughts.

"Oh…yeah, my bad," he said getting out, "I'm just hella tired."

"Why don' yuh rest fuh a while?"

"Naw, I'm good. After this meeting, I'll be able to sleep like a baby with all this money I'ma be holding," he said trying to laugh as they made their way inside.

After checking into the hotel, Jewel gave Dash and Tusan their key cards before they all went their separate ways.

Ring. Ring. Ring. Ring. Ring.

Jewel looked down at his phone again as he made his way toward the elevator. It was Sacario.

These niggas must be bored, he thought as he pressed *Ignore* again.

Jewel had to be focused. Even though he was no longer affiliated with the M.A.C. Boys as their leader, his heart never left. The attacks on the clique felt personal especially with Smackz being murdered in cold blood. He had no time to lose. The clock was ticking.

After getting settled in his suite, he decided to take a quick shower before he got ready for the meeting. He desperately wanted to scrub the airplane smell from off of his skin. Walking over to his suitcase, he pulled out the suit bag he had inside and laid it across the bed.

Ring. Ring. Ring. Ring.

Suddenly, he heard his phone ringing on the nightstand.

Man, if these niggas don't go somewhere, Jewel thought to himself, but when he looked down at the screen, he realized that it was Khailiah.

"What's up, K?" he asked sitting down in a chair that sat next to the ceiling-high window.

"Ya'll make to LA okay?"

"Yeah, I was about to start getting ready now."

"Oh…well, I'll just call you back then."

"Naw, it's good. I wanted to talk to you."

"About?"

"Look, I know that shit got kinda out of hand…"

"Kinda?"

"Okay, a lot out of hand," he laughed.

"To be honest, Jewel, I'm not even mad…at you, but fuck that bitch forreal."

"Reagan is a lot of things but a scrapper has never been one of them. I don't even know where all of that came from."

"She's your wife, J. I get it. If you were mine, I'd probably act the same way."

"Naw, I don't think you would've gone about it all like that."

"You don't know me then," she laughed, "What happened in D.R. was completely inappropriate, and I can't apologize enough. Given our work relationship, I should have known better. Reagan had every right to be upset."

"The situation is just fucked up," Jewel said shaking his head.

"What you mean?"

"You're a solid chick, Khailiah, and any dude would be lucky to have you. I just hate that we met at the wrong time, and it can't be me, you know?"

"What are you saying?" she asked, blushing a little.

"If me and Reagan didn't have our little situation, I would've wanted to pursue you."

"Jewel, shut up…"

"I'm being forreal…"

"You're just saying all this 'cause you and Reagan are going through the motions right now."

"Naw, it's deeper than that. Me and Reagan have been through a lot, and at the time, it all seemed worth it. I think I was blinded by how hard it was to tame her. She was a challenge to me."

"What…you calling me easy or something?"

"Not like that. She was wild, and I guess my ego wanted to try and control her. I've never had a female play me as much as Reagan has."

"And that was appealing to you?"

"I can't even explain it."

"So why did you get married then?"

"'Cause I do love her, and I wanted to make things right. After shit went left with my baby mama, it was like Reagan was who I was supposed to be with, but now, I'm not so sure."

"Have you talked to her?"

"Not since ya'll got into it. She tried hitting my phone a couple times, but I just stayed down at the office with Tusan going over all the details for today."

"About that…," Khailiah said as her voice shook, "I need to tell you something, and it's very…"

"Shit!" Jewel said cutting her off as he looked over at the clock, "Ay, look, if I'ma make this meeting…I gotta get my ass out of here, okay? You know how that nigga Conner gets."

"But, Jewel, it's about…"

"We'll talk as soon as I get back," he said before he ended the call.

Rushing to the bathroom, he continued his routine as he prepared himself for the day. It was time to see what Dash was really made of.

$$$$$

Forty-five minutes later, Jewel stood in front of the full-length mirror that sat against the wall as he admired himself. The Cremieux suit he wore fit his sculpted body to perfection. With a few finishing touches, he put on his diamond-encrusted cufflinks and dabbed some Tom Ford cologne on his neck and behind his ear before he headed towards the door.

Knock. Knock. Knock. Knock.

Just as he reached for the handle, there was a knock on the door. It was Tusan.

"What's up, bruh?" he said as he opened it, "I was just about to come and get you niggas. Ya'll ready?"

"Ay, can we talk fuh a few minutes?" he asked as he brushed past Jewel and made his way into the room. Another light-skinned dude with dreads longer than Tusan's followed closely behind him but didn't utter a word.

"Uh…where's Dash?"

"In his room. Mi tol' him we call him when we get done here."

"What's up?" Jewel asked sensing Tusan's urgency.

"Dis be mi brudda Remy. He pun mi team."

"Nice to meet you, bruh," he said extending his hand.

"While mi been workin' wit' yuh, he been tekin' care of shit behind de scenes, ya know?"

"Tusan mention ta me dah Dash is in GMB."

"Yeah, I mean, he was. That's the clique Kisino ran before he died. Dash and his niggas are kinda just floating out here at this point."

"Dah's not de case. GMB is alive an' well, an' Dash been a huge part of dah," Remy said looking him in the eyes.

"What does that mean?"

"Bein' from out of town, niggas no wan' ta tell mi much, but word pun de street is dah GMB was de one behind de hit. Mi heard dah de day yuh were shot at, Dash jes came back from Houston."

"Houston?" Jewel said more to himself. He knew where GMB originated, but Dash swore up and down that he had never been out of California.

"Jewel, mi know dis seems confusin'," Tusan chimed in, "but yuh were right too."

"Huh?"

"Dash no runnin' tings alone. Kisino's potnah Maxx Money took ova business in Texas. Bein' dah yuh rank has changed a lot in jes a few years, yuh been pun dere radar. Mi hate ta say it, but Dash is de opp."

Sacario was right, Jewel thought as he shook his head. He couldn't believe that he had left himself open to be vulnerable again.

"Mi bring Remy along 'cause mi wan' him ta tell yuh himself. He been followin' Dash 'round an' a few of his potnahs fuh de pas' couple weeks, an' all signs point ta GMB."

"This nigga must have a fucking death wish," Jewel said through his teeth.

"Wit' mi an' Remy here now, it be no problem fuh us ta tek care of de situation."

"Naw, I got it handled," Jewel said walking out of the room.

$$$$$

An hour later, Jewel, Dash, and Tusan arrived at a gray building with all-black windows. There was no signage anywhere, so Dash had no idea where they were.

"You cool?" Jewel asked, noticing the nervousness on his face.

"...yeah, I'm straight. This shit just feels like a set to keep it solid...that's all. I'm used to meeting niggas on the block, not the boardroom."

"Relax, bruh," he said placing his hand on his shoulder as they got out of the car, "If you decide to fuck with me, this is how shit's gon' be from now on."

"I'm ready, blood," Dash said taking a deep breath.

"Let's go then," Jewel smiled.

Just as they were about to enter the building, Jewel stopped Tusan dead in his tracks.

"Ay, hang back for me."

"Do you tink dah afta everyting mi tol' yuh dah's a good idea?" he whispered.

"I got it from here," Jewel reassured him, "I need you to do me a favor anyway."

"Wuh?" Tusan asked, becoming frustrated.

"I got a car back at the hotel," he said handing him the keys, "Have the driver take you back, and then you drive back here. I already informed the driver that we wouldn't be needing him to pick us up."

"Jewel, yuh know mi no driva, right?"

"Trust me on this," he said patting him on the back before he headed inside to meet Dash.

"Everything cool?" Dash asked as he stood off to the side by the elevators.

"Yeah, Tusan had to make a run real quick, so he's gon' pick us up after we get done here."

"Oh, okay…fa sho," he said wiping his sweaty palms off on his pant leg.

"Now, I wanted to bring you here today to show you a little bit of what I do on the regular. I know that street shit seems cool at first, but I can tell you from experience that the shit gets old quick," Jewel lied, "There's a certain ceiling you reach when you just set out to be a block boy. You gotta dream bigger than that, my nigga."

"I can dig it."

"So you just let me talk, but if you have any questions, let me know."

"It's gucci…"

Ready to finally get down to business, Jewel pressed the button to the elevator as they waited for it to reach the bottom floor. The lobby was completely empty, but Jewel knew exactly where to go. Once they got inside, he pressed the button for the fifteenth floor. No words were spoken as Jewel began to get in his zone. Despite everything that was going on around him, his main focus was still getting to the money.

Ding.

As they stepped off the elevator, Dash followed Jewel. They walked down a long corridor until they got to a small office that sat off to the right.

Knock. Knock.

Jewel waited patiently until the old, chipped wooden door slowly opened.

"Jewel!" a younger white guy in a white button-up and a dark blue blazer said in excitement.

"How you doing today, Conner?"

"Better now that you're here," he said flipping his hair out of his eye. His surfer boy haircut made it look like he should've been out on the water somewhere, not making drug deals.

"This is my associate Dash. Dash, this is Conner Brinkley."

"Nice to meet you, man," he said extending his hand.

"Likewise," Conner smiled, "Jewel, you remember Ronald and Caiden." Two of his men sat towards the back of the room never taking their eyes off Jewel.

"Of course, nice to see you gentlemen again." They just nodded. "Well, let's get down to business," Jewel said sitting down.

"You guys want some water or juice or anything?" Conner offered.

"Naw, we're good. Thanks though, bro."

"No prob…"

"Like I was saying, I know that we had come to an agreement the last time we met. You were going to test out the product, and if you were satisfied, which I know you should be, we would move forward, right?"

"For sure. Let me tell you, Jewel. Me and my guys were high for days," Conner laughed, "The shit was wild, bro."

"Well, that's what we like to hear, but I just want to make it clear that we're not in the business of selling for personal use. Our product is of the utmost quality, and in order for this deal to go through in a way that's mutually beneficial for the both of us, bulk is the only way to go."

"I wouldn't have it any other way, J Dawg. You know me, and you know Hollywood. I'm probably being conservative with my order, but I think forty-five should be enough to start off with. Between all the parties I promote, these college whores, and just traveling as much as I do, I need as much coke as I can handle, bro. Have you ever had a big tittie bleached blonde bitch snort a line off your dick in the middle of VIP?"

"I can't say that I have," Jewel laughed.

"You haven't lived then, bro. If you have the candy, the hoes will come."

"You're a wild boy, Conner."

"What about you, Dash? You look like you don't have any problems getting the ladies," he said putting his hand up for a high-five.

"…uh," Dash said looking at Jewel. Jewel nodded his head. "The club isn't really my scene. I like to stay where the money is."

"I can respect that, but you have to let loose and have some fun sometimes. All work and no play makes for a very unhappy man."

"As long as my pockets are right, I should be good," Dash smiled.

"Don't say I didn't warn you," Conner said shaking his head, "Where you from?"

"Sacramento, but I got a lot of family in Houston."

"No shit? I love Texas. You ever been to ONYX?"

"Hell yeah," Dash said relaxing a little, "I was actually out there not too long ago."

"We're going to have to link up the next time I'm out there on business," Conner winked, "These dollar bills aren't just going to throw themselves."

"You a fool," he laughed.

"I'm serious. I mean, for the most part, I'm a pretty simple guy. I like my Kates, and Kirstens, and Julies, but when it comes to strip clubs, if there isn't a female named Passion or Desire performing, I can't even entertain it. I'm there for the show, you know?"

"Oh, believe me, I know. There's nothing like a nice pair of juicy thighs and fat ass to go along with it."

"Preach, bro."

"Well, now that we've gotten to know each other a little better," Jewel said interrupting, "I say we get down to the numbers."

"You hear this dude?" Conner asked Dash, motioning toward Jewel, "He's always so serious…okay, Jewel, what are we looking at?"

"If you're looking to do forty-five a month, that'll be around $740,000."

"Let's just make it an even $750,000. That'll be easier for me to remember."

"Okay, I'll throw in an extra pack for $10,000, so that way, the numbers work out."

"You're a good man, Jewel…always looking out for me," Conner smiled, "Ay, kid, if you're really tryna make it in this game, stick close to this guy. He can take you places."

Ready to seal the deal, Conner stood up to shake Jewel and Dash's hands.

"I'm counting on it," Dash grinned.

$$$$$

After collecting the initial deposit from Conner, Jewel and Dash made their way back downstairs. Dash was beaming with excitement. He had never seen so much money in one place before, but to Jewel, it was just another day at the office.

"Ay, Jewel, are all of the connects you work with like that?"

"Hell naw," he said as they walked outside into the cool air, "Conner is a trust fund baby. He doesn't have to do any of this shit to get dough. The nigga thinks he's dude from *Malibu's Most Wanted* or something, but his money's green, so I don't say too much."

"Shit, I wouldn't either."

Suddenly, Tusan pulled up in front of them in an all-black Impala. Jewel made sure to tuck the black briefcase he held in his hand underneath the seat before he got inside.

"We headed back to the telly?" Dash asked as he jumped in the back.

"Yeah, I just got one more stop to make. Ay, take this freeway up here," Jewel instructed Tusan as he leaned his chair back.

"I ain't gon' lie, that shit was lit," he said scooting up a bit, "I see why you not on the corner anymore. That shit is easy money."

"Naw, it's not that. I just make it look easy. It takes some time getting use to though."

"You basically just have to finesse these niggas though, right?"

"Something like that," Jewel said staring out the window, "…but, ay, you never told me that you be out in Houston. I got people out there. I thought you said you've never been out of California."

"H-Town is like my second home. I guess I never really thought to count it, feel me?"

"When's the last time you've been back?"

"Shit, maybe like two-three months ago. I usually go out there to fuck with my cousin Maxx."

"That's what's up," Jewel said, clinching his fist. It was beginning to look like everything Tusan and Remy told him was actually true.

"But forreal, Jewel, thank you for bringing me out here. I was a little skeptical at first. I mean, there has been so much bad blood between our families that I really didn't know how this shit was gon' go."

"I'm a believer in second chances, feel me? I think everybody has the ability to change up especially if the opportunity is right."

"Even though shit got crazy with you and Kisino, I knew you were solid when you and your boys came to the house that day."

"What?" Jewel asked turning around.

"The night Kisino killed that Puerto Rican broad."

"Who…Asaya?"

"I think that was her name. I didn't really talk to her too much. I just remember her coming up to the house, but the bitch was working with them people. She came up in that mothafucka wearing a wire. That nigga Kisino found that shit with the quickness, and it was over after that."

"You were there?" Jewel asked in disbelief. He knew that it was a while ago, but he only remembered seeing Blue and Kisino.

"Yeah, after he snapped her neck, he had me and Blue take her upstairs to get her body out the way I guess. I was gon' come back down, but that's when we heard you and your boys come in. Me and that nigga Blue were waiting in the cuts. We honestly could've taken all of ya'll out, but after the boys came in and Kisino killed Pop, we knew it was over for him," he said lowering his head.

"You were fucking there the whole time?" Jewel asked again as his voice rose.

"I-I-I…"

"You watched them all die?" Hearing Pop's name sent Jewel over the edge. He was disgusted with himself. At that moment, he realized that he had been breaking bread with the enemy.

"Damn, nigga, you acting like I pulled the trigger or something."

"You might as well have, you bitch-ass nigga," Jewel said pulling his gun from out of his waistband and putting two to Dash's chest.

Pop. Pop.

"Fuck!" Tusan said, pulling over and parking behind an abandoned warehouse.

Dash's body slowly slumped down onto the backseat as blood oozed from the bullet holes that pierced his skin.

"This whole time the nigga was involved too," Jewel said to himself, "He watched them die. He watched Pop die! How could I have been so stupid? That nigga's been a snake." He slammed his gun over and over again against the side of his forehead as Pop's face entered his mind. "Sacario was right. I let these niggas get so close to me…I lost my cousin, my fuckin' cousin, blood. What the fuck am I supposed to tell my uncle?"

"Jewel! Jewel!" Tusan yelled, trying to distract him from his rant as he inspected his work, "Mi need yuh ta focus, okay? Yuh did wuh yuh had ta do. Dash was deadweight. He was de enemy, Jewel. Mi tek care of all dis. I jes need yuh ta chill."

Suddenly, Jewel's phone started ringing. Needing to figure out his next move, he went to press *Ignore* until he saw that it was his grandfather. He had no choice but to answer.

"Abuelo," he said trying to steady his voice.

"Nieto, I haven't heard from you since you left."

"I know…I've just been busy working, you know?"

"Working on who tried to kill you I hope."

"Yes, Abuelo, I found the mothafucka who set us up," Jewel said looking at Tusan as he dragged Dash's body from out of the car.

"Good, I'm glad that it has been taken care of especially for the sake of your primo, may he rest in peace. When I heard that it was somebody from this…"

"Abuelo, I have a situation that I gotta deal with."

"Jewel…"

"I promise to call you back as soon as I can," he said as he watched Tusan set a flame to Dash's clothes.

"Jewel, I need…" Before he could say anything else, Jewel hung up as he became mesmerized by the fire that danced off of Dash's body.

"It's done," Tusan said looking up at him as a smile spread across his face.

Chapter Thirteen

Two Days Later…

Reagan whizzed around the house trying to finish cleaning up as much as she could. It was the only thing that seemed to keep her mind off Jewel. After her altercation with Khailiah, she never expected for him to kick her out, let alone not come home. But despite all of the calls and texts she sent, she never received a response. She didn't understand how their marriage even got to this point. They used to be inseparable, but now, it felt like they were truly on the brink of divorce, and Reagan had no one to turn to. She tried to reach out to Diamond a few times, but with Hassan getting shot and their wedding continuing to be postponed, she was in her own world. As much as Diamond wanted to be there for her girl, she couldn't've cared less about Jewel's constant mood swings.

Reagan looked up at the clock and realized that it was almost 2:30 p.m.

"Fuck!" she said to herself as she continued to scrub the bathtub with Ajax. She had to pick up Chase from daycare at 3 p.m., and she knew that if she didn't hurry, she wouldn't make it in time. Putting Chase in daycare was the last thing Reagan wanted to do, but she didn't have a choice. He had been by her side since day one, but between Jewel and his disappearing acts, Laura searching for a new place, and Joe being M.I.A., she didn't have too many people she could call on to watch him throughout the day, so *Sunshine Academy* it was.

I'll just finish this shit when I get back, she thought to herself as she stood to her feet, wiping the sweat off her brow with the back of her hand. As her wedding ring slid across her face, she instantly got sad again. Staring at the flawless stone of forever Jewel had adorned her finger with now just seemed like a joke.

Ding. Dong.

Reagan looked in the mirror at the sad expression she wore as she adjusted her fitted white t-shirt. Attempting to paint a smile on her face, she made her way downstairs.

"Who is it?" she yelled.

Ding. Dong.

"Who the fuck is...," she said as she flung the door open, "Tusan?"

"Sorry ta jes pop up like dis," he smiled.

"It's good...but Jewel's not here though."

"Mi know. We jes got back from LA."

"LA?"

"Yeah, he had some business ta tek care of out dere. He no tell yuh?"

"Of course not," she said rolling her eyes, "That nigga never tells me shit. Anyway, I was just about to go pick up my son from daycare, but..."

"Mi can tek yuh if yuh wan'."

"You sure? I wouldn't want to make you go out of your way."

"Naw, it's good. Mi needed ta talk ta yuh anyway."

"Okay, let me just go grab my purse right quick," she said running back into the house, closing the door behind her.

Before she grabbed her purse from off of the couch in the living room, she walked into the bathroom downstairs and splashed some water throughout her curly hair, put some edge control on her edges, and threw her hair up into a bun. She didn't have much time to do anything else.

"Why am I tripping?" she asked herself. Even though she didn't know too much about Tusan, she had to admit that he was sexy as hell, and every time he was around, she seemed to get butterflies in her stomach. "You're just going to get Chase," she had to remind herself, "That's it...that's all."

Opting out of a full-face off makeup, she decided to just throw on a coat of *Angel* M.A.C. lipglass and some eye liner and mascara. Checking herself one last time in the mirror, she figured she looked decent enough to finally leave. After grabbing her purse, she was out the door.

"My bad," she said as she walked outside up to Tusan's truck.

"No problem…mi got all de time in de world ta wait fuh a pretty gyal like yuh."

"Well, thanks for the ride," she said trying not to blush.

"It's de leas' mi can do," he said unable to take his eyes off her.

"Listen, Tusan, I know you work for Jewel and all, but I don't need babysitting, okay? I do perfectly fine on my own. Whatever Jewel has going on, that's him."

"Dah's not why mi here," he admitted.

"Then what's up?"

"Mi jes wan' ta check pun yuh…when mi saw yuh down at Jewel's office, mi could tell dah yuh didn't know 'bout him an' Khailiah."

Hearing her name had Reagan ready to go over the edge again, but she did her best to keep her composure.

"Me and Jewel have been together for a while now, and even though we don't have any kids together, we still share a family, you know?"

"Mi can imagine dah it's hard ta jes leh all dah go, but from weh mi sittin', yuh deserve betta dan dah."

"But you don't even know me," she laughed, "How would you know what I deserve?"

"Mi very perceptive even when yuh no tink mi watchin'."

"Well, thank you," she smiled, "Jewel's not perfect by a long shot but neither am I. We have a lot to work on, but that's what marriage is for, right?"

"Mi neva been married, so mi no know how it's 'sposed to be, but if yuh were mi wife, mi couldn't even imagine cheatin' pun yuh."

"You're gonna get off at the next exit," she said pointing ahead as he continued to drive, "Jewel said that it was only a kiss, so…"

"An' yuh believe him?"

"Do I have a choice?"

"Yuh always have a choice…listen, mi no wan' ta get in ya business, but from wuh mi seen it's a lot mo' between Jewel an' Khailiah dan he would like ta leh on."

"Really?" Reagan asked in disbelief.

"Mi offered ta give him a ride home, but when we land, dere she was."

Reagan put her head down as she tried to process the news. *Is he really fucking this bitch behind my back?* she thought to herself. Whatever was going on between them, she had every intention on finding out exactly what it was. She was tired of waiting for Jewel to be honest with her. At this point, it seemed like he was incapable of telling the truth anymore.

"Why are you telling me all this?" she asked turning to face him.

"Like mi said befo', mi know it's none of mi business, but mi can tell dah yuh are a good woman. Weh mi come from, family means everyting, an' mi jes tink dah Jewel has lost sight of dah. Mi don' know wuh yuh relationship was like befo', but right now, it jes seems like he tekin' yuh fuh granted," Tusan said placing his hand on top of hers as he caressed her skin with his thumb, "An' ta mi, yuh deserve ta be cherish."

$$$$$

"Jewel, you know you could stay at a hotel, right?" Khailiah asked holding the front door open for him.

"Yeah, I could," he smiled, "But why would I want to do that?"

After returning from LA, Jewel called Khailiah to come and pick him up. He could've gotten a ride with Tusan and went back home, but after watching Dash's body burn to ashes, he just wanted to get away from it all.

"You going home after this?" she asked as he picked up his suitcase, preparing to leave.

"I don't know…"

"What do you mean you don't know?"

"I'm not sure where I want to be right now," he admitted.

"Jewel, you have a wife and kids. I know that shit seems rocky right now, but you have to go home eventually. You can't run away from your problems forever."

"I'm not running though. I know how this shit looks, but I'm not tryna use you as a rebound or nothing like that."

"Yeah, I know 'cause you are mar…ried."

"I've been thinking a lot about that."

"And?" Khailiah asked as her curiosity peaked.

"I think I want to separate for a while…at least until I figure all this shit out, you know?"

"Jewel, you don't mean that."

"I do though. At this point in my life, I'm convinced that me and Reagan are just on two different pages right now. I love her, and I love Chase with everything I have in me…that's never gonna change, but

I'm tired of being unhappy every day. It's like no matter what I do, I can't make shit right between us."

"Maybe it's just gonna take some time."

"Man, I don't have time like that…life's too short."

Khailiah didn't know what to say. She had been waiting for over a year to hear these words come from Jewel, but she wondered if it was too late for them.

"Well, you know you can stay here for as long as you need to, J."

"Thank you, Khailiah. I really appreciate you, you know that? Not a lot of women would've put up with half of this shit."

"What are friends for?"

"You're more to me than just a friend," he said kissing her softly. Chills ran throughout her body as he caressed the side of her face. She melted into his embrace, never wanting the moment to end.

"You coming back tonight?" she asked finally pulling away from him, trying to catch her breath.

"We'll see…I gotta link up with Sacario and Hassan later. I'll hit you though."

"K," she smiled.

"Oh, before I forget, I got you something."

"What?"

"It's nothing too much," he said digging in the side of his bag, "I just wanted to get you something to say thank you."

"Thank you for what?"

"For just being there. Like you said, Reagan doesn't have my back, and I'm starting to realize that it's been like that since day one. Anything that I'm doing, she's against it, but I always thought that it was because she was just looking out for a nigga, but she really just wants to control me."

"Jewel, I…"

"You don't have to say anything. I wanted to do this," he said pulling out a long, black box. When he lifted the lid, Khailiah was speechless. Inside sat a two-carat yellow and white diamond, heart-shaped, white gold necklace.

"It's beautiful, Jewel," she said tracing the diamonds with her finger.

"You mean a lot to me, and I hope that this shows you just a little of how much."

"How much did it cost?" she asked in amazement. The shine coming from the stones was almost blinding.

"Bands, girl," he laughed, "But that shit don't even matter to me. Do you like it?"

"Like it? Jewel, I love it," she squealed as she wrapped her arms around his waist, laying her head against his chest.

"Good."

"Thank you so much," she said looking up at him, "Put it on me!"

Jewel pulled the necklace out of the box, unhooked the clasp, and gently wrapped it around Khailiah's neck. The cold sensation of the metal against her skin gave her goose bumps as the pendent slid down the middle of her chest.

"You got me feeling like I'm in high school and shit," she blushed.

"This is just a token of my appreciation for you," he said kissing her cheek, "We'll talk more later though. I gotta go before I don't get nothing done today."

As Jewel walked outside to his car, Khailiah stood in the doorway imagining what their lives would be like if they could truly be together. Everything was perfect, and she intended on it staying that way.

"I love you, Jewel Sanchez," she said playing with the diamond heart pendant with her fingers, "And I'm not gonna let nothing or nobody take that away from me."

$$$$$

Before Khailiah took Jewel back to her house, she stopped by his office, so he could pick up his car. Even though he planned on spending the night with her, he knew he had business to take care of and couldn't be stuck at her house all day. Sacario and Hassan had been blowing up his phone non-stop over the past two days, but what Jewel needed to talk about couldn't be discussed over the phone.

As he backed out of her driveway, he pulled his cellphone out of his pocket to tap in with Sacario when he realized that Laura was calling.

"What's up, Ma?" he asked, placing the phone between his ear and shoulder as he continued to reverse.

"Jewel, where are you?"

"On my way to handle some business. Why, what's up?"

"We need to talk."

"I'll be home a little later. Can it wait?"

"No."

"Ma, I…"

"Jewel your uncle Stevin just arrived. We need to talk now."

He knew that he was going to have to answer for what happened to Smackz sooner or later, but he didn't know if he was ready just yet.

"Okay…I'm on my way home now," Jewel said making a U-turn.

"No need."

"What?"

"There's no need for you to go home."

"And why not?"

"Because I'm not there. I closed on my house. You can meet us here."

"House? Why didn't you tell me that you were moving already?"

"Jewel, you've been in your own little world lately, and I didn't want to bother you. You didn't think I would be staying with you and Reagan forever, did you?" she laughed, "That wife of yours is becoming intolerable. All she does is mope around the house all day. I love you and the boys and all, but you can't expect me to suffer just because you have to."

The truth was that Laura was hurt that Joe still hadn't made his intentions clear. She had no idea where they stood, and it was driving her crazy. Not wanting to take the chance of him just popping up at Jewel's, she decided to take her house search a little more seriously. The place was smaller than she was used to, but she figured that it would do while she was in town.

"So where is this place at?" Jewel asked, not wanting to feed into his mother's dramatics.

"Elk Grove…I'll text you the address."

"Okay," he said getting ready to hang up.

"Jewel…," Laura said just before he could.

"Yeah?"

"Please come straight here. Your uncle and I don't have time for your little pit stops today."

"I'm on my way now," he sighed before finally hanging up. Jewel hurried to get to his mother's house as he prepared himself to talk to his uncle. Smackz meant everything to Stevin, and Jewel had no idea how he was going to explain how he lost his life under his watch.

I gotta go tap in with my mom right quick. You still in Sac? Jewel texted Sacario.

…

He waited for his response.

Yep. We at the house right now. Just come through when you get done.

Thirty minutes later, Jewel pulled up in front of Laura's new house. As he parked along the street, he admired the freshly manicured grass that surrounded the estate. It was so much smaller than what she had in Barbados, but it was beautiful nonetheless. Walking up the driveway, Jewel passed by a white Ferrari that was parked in the driveway. He knew it had to be Stevin's. Taking a deep breath as he walked towards the door, he knew there was no turning back.

Ding. Dong. The melodic sound echoed throughout the house as Jewel waited for his mother to answer. A few seconds later, Kurt, Laura's right-hand, came to the door.

"Jewel, how are you?"

"Good, man, what are you doing out here?" he asked as he followed him inside.

"Well, when your mother called me, I decided to come out here to help get her settled."

"She always got you working, huh?" Jewel asked, slapping him on the back.

"It's never work helping Miss Laurie," Kurt smiled.

"That's what's up," he said looking around the almost empty house, "Where is she anyway?"

"She's in the study with your uncle. Should I announce your arrival?"

"Naw, it's good," Jewel said not needing him to go through all the trouble, "You can just show me where it is."

"Right this way."

As they walked down a narrow hallway, Jewel's nerves were on edge. He tried to go over what he was going to say to Stevin in his head, but he had nothing.

"They're right through there," Kurt said motioning towards the door that sat in front of them, "Do you require anything else?"

"Nope," Jewel said sliding his hand over his face, "I think I got it from here."

Knock. Knock. Knock.

"Come in, Jewel," Laura said from behind the door.

"What's going on, Ma?" he asked, walking into the room. He immediately saw Stevin, but he did his best to avoid eye contact.

"How are you doing, son?" she asked as he gave her a kiss on the cheek.

"I'm hanging in there," Jewel said walking across the room, "How you doing, Unc?"

"I've been better, nephew," Stevin said standing up to give him a hug.

"Jewel, the reason you're here today is most likely obvious," Laura started.

"Yeah, for the most part," he said putting his head down.

"What happened, Jewel?" Stevin asked needing answers, "The shit just doesn't make any sense."

"Listen, Unc, losing Smackz…losing Smackz was the last thing I would have ever wanted to see happen, but I wasn't there."

"That doesn't explain why my son is dead," he snapped.

"I know, and I blame myself. Everything was going smooth. We had the product right. Money was coming in faster than we knew what to do with. For the first time, I felt like Smackz had everything under control. I know my mom told you about me and my little sister getting popped at in front of my office."

"Yeah, she mentioned it."

"Well, I thought that they were after me, but after Smackz got killed, it was clear that these niggas were after the M.A.C. Boys."

"Who?"

"GMB. Some of the members of Kisino's clique were plotting on the M.A.C. Boys as retaliation for his death I'm assuming. One of his main niggas came down to the office and said that GMB wanted to link up with us and get this money."

"And what did you say?"

"I said, yeah," Jewel said lowering his gaze. He knew he was responsible for his cousin being murdered, and it was something he was going to have to take to his grave.

"You said yeah?" Stevin questioned.

"At the time, I didn't put two-and-two together. They seemed like they could've been beneficial."

"Jewel, please don't tell me that you're that stupid," he yelled, "This is who we put in charge of our whole operation, Laurie?"

"Listen, Unc, I know I fucked up, but I'm still not sure how these niggas got into the lab. Smackz had that bitch locked down from day one."

"Does it fucking matter?"

"I know that there's nothing I can say to make this better, to make him come back, but I need you to know that the situation has been handled…permanently. I wasn't just about to let that shit go."

"That doesn't bring my son back, Jewel," Stevin said slamming his fist down on the coffee table in front of him, "My son's ashes are sitting in a fucking jar right now."

"What?"

"We had Stevin cremated. Your aunt is sick behind this. She can barely get out of bed. As bad as it hurt me to do this, I had him cremated," he said picking up Smackz's urn, "I know it sounds crazy, but I need to have something to hold on to, you know?"

"Unc, you have to believe me. Once I found out about GMB, I took care of it."

"Jewel," Stevin sighed, "We're blood, and nothing can change that. I know that you would have never intentionally put Stevin Jr. in harm's way. Nonetheless, what's done is done," he said gliding his hand across the solid gold container that would forever be home to his son's remains, "But now, you have to protect yourself."

"Like I said, I took care of it."

"And plus, Jewel has security now," Laura chimed in.

"Security?"

"Yes, you remember Jovan, right?"

"Of course, how could I forget that snake-ass mothafucka?"

"Stevin, please, language…"

"Jovan was Tusan's dad, right?" Jewel asked.

"Please don't tell me that's who you have working for you," Stevin said shaking his head.

"That was in the past, Stevie."

"Fuck all that! Once a thief, always a thief, and I'm pretty sure his son is no different."

"What do you mean, Unc?" Jewel was curious by their exchange. Tusan never said too much about his father.

"Nothing, Jewel, it's all hearsay…"

"Back when your mother and I first started out, your grandfather insisted that we have someone to look out for us. We were dealing with a lot of money, and of course enemies always come along with that. Jovan was recommended by a friend of the family, so immediately we trusted him like he *was* family. He and his men came with us everywhere. It was like we had our own secret service or some shit. Jovan had men looking over our homes, our family, everything. Our every move was always under watch."

"That's what we were paying them for," Laura snapped.

"Yeah, but we weren't paying them to rob us from right under our nose."

"What do you mean?"

"Over the years, Jovan had to have stolen over $1 million from our family."

"And you never caught him? That's a lot of money to just go unnoticed."

"I was suspicious, and I let Papa know, but after he died, Jovan seemed to somehow convince your mother that the numbers were right, but I knew better."

"No, he never told me that. He said that many of our 'friends' had been taking advantage of us for years. We just never noticed because we wanted to take care of everyone. It was all speculation though. Jovan was a very simple man. He was *honest* and *hardworking*. I just couldn't imagine that he would steal from us, not after all Papa had done for him."

"And now you have his son continuing the tradition I see."

"Tusan is a good boy."

"He's the son of a snake, Laurie. Why would you bring him around our family? After Jovan was killed, I thought I had gotten rid of the Coles once and for all."

"Stevin, please trust me, okay? I'm not as moronic as you believe me to be. If Jovan ever proved himself to be untrustworthy, I wouldn't have thought twice about hiring his son."

"Yeah, Unc, I don't know too much about this Jovan guy, but Tusan is as solid as they come. He was the one who was there when Smackz died. He did his best to hold them niggas back, but they were outnumbered. He helped me dispose of the nigga who set up this whole thing, so in my mind, he's good people." Jewel was convinced.

"You're just like ya mama," Stevin said shaking his head again, "Sometimes, your grass is so high, you can't see the snakes coming, but believe me, nephew, you have one right in front of your face. Please just watch your back."

Chapter Fourteen

After tying up a few loose ends with his uncle, Jewel decided to head over to Hassan's to meet up with him and Sacario. As he continued to drive, he couldn't get Stevin's words out of his head.

"Sometimes, your grass is so high, you can't see the snakes coming, but believe me, nephew, you have one right in front of your face."

There's no way Tusan is an opp, he thought to himself, *My mom wouldn't do no shit like that.* He tried to shake the thought from his mind, but it was hard. There was obvious tension between Stevin and the Cole family, and it seemed like it had to do with a lot more than just money.

"Í don't have time for this shit," Jewel said to himself, shaking his head.

Twenty minutes later, he pulled up in front of Hassan's house. He parked right behind Sacario's midnight blue Regal on 24s before he hopped out with a smile spread across his face. The sun was shining, Dash was gone, and everything was right in the world again.

Ding. Dong.

As Jewel waited for someone to answer, his phone started to vibrate in his pocket. Pulling it out, he saw that he had a text from Khailiah.

Hey, I know you're busy and all, but I really hope you'll be able to make it back tonight. There's something that I really have to talk to you about, and it can't wait anymore.

"Took you long enough, nigga," K-2 said, swinging the door open.

"...ay, what you doing out here, bruh?" Jewel asked, quickly putting his phone back in his pocket.

"You know me, blood. Once I heard there was trouble in paradise, I had to get out here quick."

"Sacario told you?" Jewel asked, scratching the back of his head. Just like Sacario, he wanted to shield K-2 away from the street life they both decided to still live. Jewel was proud of K-2 and his decision to leave the game alone, and he refused to let anything jeopardize that for his sister's sake.

"Naw, that's the cold part. The streets are talking though," K-2 said leading them into the living room.

"I bet," Jewel smiled, knowing that he had already taken care of the situation.

"What's up, bruh?" Hassan asked as they entered the room.

"Ain't nothing. How you feeling?"

"I'm cool. I still can't really move my arm around too much, but it's better than it was."

"You go to the doctors yet?"

"Hell naw, and I don't plan to. You know they don't take gunshot wounds lightly, bruh. I ain't even tryna to get into all that right now."

"Yeah, but you don't want to fuck around and have that mothafucka be paralyzed."

"I'll manage," Hassan laughed, "That's what I have Diamond for, right?"

"Speaking of Diamond, where she at?"

"Her and Jailen went to the movies. I told her that I needed to handle some business right quick."

"Oh, okay," Jewel said relaxing a little bit, knowing that his son wasn't there, "I need to link up with her later…so, anyway, what ya'll been blowing me up for? What's up?"

"Where'd you disappear to?" Sacario asked.

"I went to see Conner…I closed that deal with hm. He's in for like forty-five a month."

"That's what's up," Hassan said.

"Why you couldn't answer the phone though?" Sacario questioned.

"Nigga, you sound like Reagan right now," Jewel laughed, "Chill, bruh."

"Blood, I'm being serious."

"Shit, me too. I couldn't answer because I had some other business to tend to."

"Like?"

"Like Dash."

"Dash?"

"Yeah, I thought about what you said, and shit wasn't adding up, but it really started to get funky when Tusan let me know that Dash and GMB were still in operation. He apparently had been going back and forth between Sac and Houston to link up with this nigga named Maxx Money. That's when they took out the hit. It was all on some get-back shit for Kisino being killed."

"But we had nothing to do with that," K-2 chimed in, "Vanessa smoked that nigga."

"I know," Jewel said.

"And all this information came from Tusan?"

"Well, yeah, him and his brother Remy. Before we went to see Conner, they laced me."

"And this Remy nigga just showed up, or he came with ya'll?" Hassan asked.

"He came a little later after we got there."

"And what did Dash have to say about all this?"

"I closed the deal with Conner first, but as we were sitting there, I started putting two-and-two together. Dash was a rat, and I invited him and his team to infiltrate the M.A.C. Boys."

"Jewel, whoever made that hit had inside information. How the fuck would Dash and some random nigga in Houston know our entire operation?"

"Why you changing the story now?" Jewel asked confused, "The last time I checked, you were convinced that Dash and GMB were the ones behind all this shit."

"I know, but…I was wrong," Sacario admitted.

"What?"

"Listen, J, word on the street is that the niggas who did this were some out-of-town niggas," K-2 said.

"Yeah…Houston."

"No…I mean, *waaaaayyy* out of town, like from Jamaica or somewhere like that."

"I don't understand," Jewel said scratching his head.

"You remember Nick from Oak Park?"

"The tall, light-skinned one who used to have dreads?"

"Yeah."

"What about him?"

"He came down to the shop the other day to get cut, and I was slappin' Serg's new CD."

"Okay…"

"He was like, 'That shit go! Who's that?' After I told him it was Serg, he had this dumb-ass look on his face. He said he thought whoever hit the M.A.C. Boys had put us out of commission. Now mind you, you niggas don't tell me shit, so I'm completely in the dark, feel me? Nick wasn't tryna say too much at first 'cause I know he could tell that I didn't know shit, but I pressed his ass. That's when he finally said that he heard that it was some Jamaicans."

"That's crazy as fuck," Jewel laughed, "Ain't no Jamaican niggas ever been on the radar, so why all of a sudden? Like Sacario said, Dash came out of nowhere, and then the next day, the warehouse gets hit and Smackz gets popped. It can't just be a coincidence."

"That's what I thought at first, but then I really started to evaluate the situation. Who else just fucking came out of nowhere?"

"Who?" Jewel asked oblivious.

"Tusan," Sacario said looking Jewel right in the eyes, "Think about his accent, bruh. It would be easy for niggas to mistake him for Jamaican."

"Man, go on with that shit. You sound just like my uncle right now."

"What?"

"Before I slid over here, I went to go see him. He's in town from Florida. I hadn't really talked to him ever since he found out that Smackz was killed, but I knew he was gonna want some answers, and I finally had them to give. I told him that Dash had been taken care of, that he was one the one who set up Smackz to be murdered. He seemed convinced at first until my mom brought up Tusan."

"What he say?"

"I guess he had beef with Tusan's dad or something. Word was going around that he was stealing money from my grandfather, and Unc obviously didn't like that shit. When I told him that Tusan seemed cool, he told me to watch my back."

"See, nigga, it's not just us. Your uncle's been knowing this nigga, but we just met him."

"But my mom brought him on. Why would she throw an opp into the mix?"

"Maybe she doesn't know this nigga's real get down."

"Naw, 'cause after I started asking Dash about his affiliations, he admitted that he still fucks with GMB and he just came back from Houston."

"Jewel, I'm telling you it wasn't him. Tusan was trained to see and hear everything, so it's not farfetched to think that he could've learned the ins and outs on how we operate…with some help though. I don't know who the leak is, but the nigga is working with somebody. You got this man around you, your house, your family. I don't know what the fuck he wants, but, Jewel, you have to believe me when I say that he's gonna strike again. We just don't know when. I know I was wrong when I said it was Dash, but everything right now is pointing to Tusan. Watch that nigga."

Without saying a word, Jewel got up and headed outside. He needed some air.

"J," K-2 called out to him, but Sacario held him back. "Man, fuck all that," he said following Jewel's steps outside, "Jewel!"

"I'm good, bro," Jewel said, finally turning around, "If everything ya'll saying is true, then I need to be at the hut. I've had this nigga in my house, around Reagan, around my kids…I gotta figure this shit out."

"Ay, big dawg, I know you got it," K-2 said patting him on the chest, "but I need to holla at you about something else."

"Nigga, there's more?" Jewel asked in disbelief as he rubbed his hand across his face again, "What now?"

"It's about Gabrielle," he admitted.

"Huh?" Jewel asked with his face screwed up, "Is she cool?" With the way things were going, nothing could surprise him anymore.

"Yeah, she's good…well, I mean, she's alive if that's what you meant, but she's really fucked up behind this Joe and Laura shit."

"So what she was saying before was forreal?"

"Yeah, unfortunately, she walked in on Joe and your mom getting it in, and ever since then, she ain't been the same."

"Damn," Jewel said staring down at the concrete. He never thought he'd see the day when his mom and dad would ever get back together. They were like poison to each other. "What you need from me though?"

"I need you to talk to her."

"Man…"

"I know shit is hectic right now, but do a nigga a solid. My life has been hell ever since this shit happened. She feels like you had something to do with it or like you knew or something."

"On mamas, I ain't know nothing."

"Nigga, that's what I told her. I was like, 'that's not even bruh's style,' but she feels like since we're homies, I'm just covering for you."

"You know my mama ain't gon' tell me no shit like that, and now that I think about it, Pop's been M.I.A. like a mothafucka. Now, I know why."

"So will you holla at her for me?"

"Do I have a choice?"

"Naw, not really," K-2 laughed, "I love Gabby and everything, but something's gotta give. She feels like she got cheated on or something, and I can't have that."

"I'll handle it, bruh," Jewel said giving him dap before he walked towards his car.

"Good looking, nigga," he said as he ran back inside the house.

When Jewel got into his car, his mind was going a mile a minute, and he couldn't slow down his thoughts. Talking to Gabrielle was the last thing he wanted to do, but he figured it would give him time to think about something else…at least for a little while. Taking a deep breath, he dialed her number.

Ring. Ring. Ring. Ring. Jewel sat there as the rings echoed throughout his car. *Ring. Ring. Ring. Ring.*

Man, fuck this, he thought.

Just as he was about to hang up, Gabrielle finally answered.

"Hello?" she asked with an attitude.

"What's up, stranger?" he asked trying to break the ice. Even over the phone, he could feel the cold shoulder she was already giving him.

"What do you want, Jewel?"

"What's all the attitude for?"

"I'm just tryna figure out why you're calling my phone."

"'Cause your my fucking sister, and I wanted to talk to yo' punk-ass."

"Uhmmmm…"

"Listen, I talked to K, and he filled me in about what's been going on lately."

"Filled you in?" she asked smacking her lips, "Nigga, I let you know about ya hoe-ass mama that night I came to your house."

"I know, Gabby, but I had a lot going on then, and who my mama is or is not fucking was not one of them."

"I just…"

"I know that you think I knew or that I set the shit up, but I swear to you I didn't. Joe and my mama kept that shit under wraps forreal forreal."

"They were fucking in your house, Jewel," she yelled, "What you mean you didn't know?"

"Man, like I said, I didn't know. I don't be there all like that, and plus, the only reason why my mama was even at the house was because she was looking for a place of her own out this way. I just found out today that she got a house in Elk Grove. Believe me, I have a lot of other shit to do with my time than to play matchmaker with other grown mothafuckas. I know you're hurt…I mean, Joe being with your mom is all you know. I get it, but I'm telling you that him getting back together with my mom is the last thing that's about to happen. They got divorced for a reason, feel me?"

"If they did…I don't even know what I would do. I would never be able to look at him the same again…or you," she confessed.

"Me? What did I do?"

"How could I just be okay knowing that my dad has a legit family on the side?"

"I had to."

$$$$$

Since her new house was in no condition to entertain any guests, Laura decided to put Stevin up in a suite close by. She was having new furniture flown in from overseas, but she wanted her brother to be more than comfortable while he was in town. Her heart ached for him. She knew that after losing Stevin Jr., he would never be the same again. She thought about the dangers she had thrusted her own son into, and even though she knew exactly what his life entailed, she couldn't imagine losing him at the hands of someone else.

As her thoughts continued to consume her on her way home, she decided to make a quick stop. It was finally time for her to face her demons. She couldn't escape them anymore.

"Kurt," she said, pressing the call-button in the back of the car.

"Yes, Miss Laurie?"

"I need you to stop somewhere before we head back to the house."

"And where would that be?"

"Joseph's house…the address should still be in the GPS system."

"Got it. We're headed there now."

Ever since their last encounter, Laura had done her best to avoid Joe at all costs. She ignored every phone call and text message he sent, and when he would periodically pop up at Jewel's house looking for her, she would have Reagan lie and say that she wasn't there. It soon became imperative that she get her own place. She felt humiliated.

When Joe left her, she didn't know how she was ever going to go on without him. Over the years, that sadness turned into hate. She despised Joe and swore that he would never get away with his betrayal, but when he showed up in Barbados and his lips met hers, all of those bad memories just washed away. It was like they were them again…before the lying, before the infidelities. Their love had returned, and Laura became drunk from it. Intoxicated by his words, she forgot about his relationship with Isabella until he made it clear that he had no idea where he really wanted to be. Not willing to be rejected again for the second time, Laura was ready to lay everything out on the table. She was nobody's secret.

Forty-five minutes later, they arrived at Joe's house. She didn't see his car parked outside, so she figured it must've been in the garage.

"Do you need me to come in with you, Miss Laurie?"

"No, that's quite alright, Kurt. I shouldn't be very long. You can go if you have other things to tend to. I can just call you when I finish up here."

"I will be right out here when you return," he said, smiling into the rearview mirror.

It's now or never, Laura thought as she took a deep breath. Before she got out of the car, she grabbed her all-white Hermès bag and headed for the front door.

Ding. Dong.

As she waited for Joe to answer, she slid off her Chanel sunglasses from on top of her jet-black, silky bob and placed them into the side pocket of her bag. As soon as she looked up, there was Isabella standing right in front of her with her arms folded across her chest.

"What the fuck are you doing here?" she snapped.

"Calm down, Isabelle. I came to see Joseph. Is he here?"

"Are you fucking serious right now?" she asked in disbelief.

"Excuse me?"

"You mean to tell me that not only are you creeping around with my husband, but you also have the audacity to show up to my home looking for him?"

"I just came to talk."

"Well, he's not here…but you should know that," Isabella said slamming the door in her face.

Ding. Dong. Ding. Dong.

"…what?" she asked swinging the door open wildly.

"Listen, like I said, I just came to talk."

"You must think I'm stupid. Bitch, I have nothing to say to you," Isabella spat.

"Just five minutes?"

Realizing that she wasn't going to be able to get rid of Laura that easily, against her better judgment, she stood to the side, allowing her to enter.

"Your five minutes start now," she said looking down at her watch.

"Is there somewhere we can sit?" Laura asked looking around the house disapprovingly.

"Would you like some fucking tea too?" Isabella asked, rolling her eyes.

"Well, I guess we'll just stand like two commoners then," she said adjusting her oversized bag over her small shoulder.

"What do you want?"

"I came to see Joseph. He has been calling and texting me for the past few days, but I haven't answered...at the time, I didn't know what to say."

"Typical," Isabella said shaking her head.

"I know that you finding out about us the way you did must've hurt…"

"Hurt? You have no idea how I feel, so cut the shit, Laura."

"But, oh, I do. How quick we forget that I was once in the same situation you find yourself in right now."

"This is not the same thing at all. Joe and I love each other. We're not just in some financial marital arrangement. He chose to be with me."

"I can only imagine the things he told you to make you be okay with being the other woman, but I can almost guarantee that it was *all* bullshit. Yes, Joseph and I were married for the sake of our family's financial wellbeing. By unifying, we were able to ensure that our children's children's children will never have to want for anything, but even before all of that, we were together. We have known each other since childhood. He was my first kiss, my first love, my first everything. He gave me a beautiful son, a beautiful life…until all that changed one day."

"And that's my fault, right?"

"I used to blame you for why he turned his back on everything he'd ever known, but now, I realize that it was wrong of me to do that. Joseph was a grown man, and he made the decision to end our marriage because we both weren't happy anymore. Although there was love there, he was evolving into a man I didn't even recognize. When he left, I was devastated. It was like my entire world came crashing down at my feet, and all I could focus on was you."

"So what…this is some get-back type shit?"

"At first…yes. I wanted to hurt you like I felt you hurt me. You knew he was married. You knew we had a child together, and yet, that didn't deter you."

"He told me that you two were over," Isabella said hanging her head.

"Of course he did, but I'm sure he didn't tell you that when he wasn't with you, he would come back home and beg for us to get back together. He used to say that you were a mistake, and he wanted to be there for his family…"

"You're lying," she said shaking her head, not wanting to hear anymore.

"Sweetheart, I have no reason to lie," Laura smirked, "At first, I believed him…I had to believe him for the survival of our family, but with every late night or every night that I slept alone, it was obvious that it was over. I tried to hold on to our dying relationship for as long as I could before I realized it had truly expired, but just know that how you feel right now is exactly how I felt fifteen years ago. It was like the rug had been pulled from underneath me."

"I never meant to break up your family, Laura," Isabella confessed, "When I met Joe, he made it seem like you two were already separated and getting ready to divorce. I didn't realize that you were still married until I began to ask about Jewel. I figured that if we were going to be together then I should meet his son, but every time, he always had an excuse of why I couldn't, or if I did, it was only down at the office. Even when I got pregnant with Gabrielle, I felt like he did everything in his power to keep her a secret in fear of disappointing you and his father. After we got married, I still felt like the other woman."

"It was obvious then that Joseph didn't know where he wanted to be. Not to make any excuses for him, but back then, he was stuck between two completely different worlds—one that was chosen and predestined for him since birth and one he felt like he had chosen on his own. That's why I'm here."

"What do you mean?"

"During our last conversation, Joseph said again that he didn't know where he wanted to be. At first, I was hurt because it was like history was repeating itself, but the more I thought about it, the less it made sense to me. Joseph knows exactly where he wants to be…and that's here with you. Despite what happened between us, I know he truly loves you."

"What?"

"When Joseph came down to Barbados, I just think that we got caught up in the nostalgia of it all. In so many ways, he was like a stranger to me, but for a brief moment, I saw a glimmer of the man I had fallen in love with, and I thought I wanted that back."

"Thought?"

"Yes, Joseph is not the same man I fell in love with, and that's okay because I believe he was intended for you. Don't get me wrong, I will love him until the day I die, but I am no longer holding on to the hope of us one day getting back together. I realize that our time together was fleeting, but it was meaningful. He gave me my son who I adore, but at this point, it's time for us both to move on and finally close this chapter in our lives."

"What brought all this on?" Isabella asked in amazement. She never imagined that she would be having a civil conversation with Laura, let alone coming to terms with their past indiscretions.

"Nothing made me happier than knowing that I was putting you through the pain that I had to endure until I remembered what that pain actually felt like, and if I couldn't respect you as a woman for sleeping with my husband knowing that we were married, how could I look myself in the mirror every day? I know that Joseph was just trying to make things better between us in a way, but this was the wrong way to go about it. When your daughter approached me, I saw the pain in her eyes, and I realized that my actions were affecting more than just me, and the last thing I ever wanted to do was involve the kids in all this mess, so I apologize. I don't know what the situation is like between you and Joseph right now, but if you still love him like I know you do, I would say just give him another chance. Everyone makes mistakes, but despite his flaws, he is a good man, and you've helped to ensure that, Isabella," Laura said walking back towards the front door, "Well, I guess my five minutes are up now, so I'll get going."

"…Laura?" she said, stopping her before she could walk outside.

"Yes?"

"Thank you," she smiled.

"For what?" Laura chuckled.

"For this. I don't think that I ever put myself in your shoes before until now because I never had to. I know it sounds selfish, but Joe shielded me from ever having to accept that I was the *other* woman. I never meant to cause more strain on your relationship with him. I was just a woman who fell in love with a man who I thought loved me too, only me."

"Like I said, we all make mistakes," Laura smiled before continuing to walk back to her car.

Chapter Fifteen

We need to talk.

Joe looked down at his phone and read the text message he had received from Isabella over and over again. It had been a few days since they had seen each other, and he wanted nothing more than to just go home. Although, he didn't regret the time he had spent with Laura, he realized that he wasn't ready to give up on his marriage with Isabella just yet. He loved her, and he was willing to do anything to get her back.

Not knowing what to expect, he decided to leave his stuff in the room again as he prepared to leave.

Is it okay if I come to the house? he texted back.

Yes, do you have time to come now?

I'm on my way.

Grabbing his keys from off of the nightstand, Joe made his way downstairs. As much as he wanted to be optimistic, he knew he had hurt Isabella more than he could've ever imagined. He just hoped that it wasn't too late to make things right again.

An hour later, Joe pulled into his driveway. Determined to have Isabella hear him out this time, he put his nerves aside and made his way towards the front door. As he placed his keys inside the lock, it didn't take him long to figure out that they had been changed. All he could do was shake his head.

Knock. Knock. Knock.

"I see you got the locks changed, huh?" he asked as Isabella quickly opened the door.

"Yeah, the day after you left actually."

"Left? You kicked me out, remember?" he laughed.

"Come in, Joe," she said, clearing a path for him to enter.

Not wanting to argue, he took a deep breath as he walked inside.

"So what did you want to talk about?" he asked, noticing his belongings boxed up in the hallway.

"Us," she said leading him into the living room.

"Listen," he said beginning to panic, "I know that I messed up, but are you really ready to just give up on our marriage, Izzy?"

"Joe, please sit down."

His nerves had him sick, but he slowly sat down on the edge of the couch as Isabella did the same.

"I know that from the locks being changed and your stuff being packed, it wouldn't take a rocket scientist to know where my mind was."

"Izzy…"

"Joe, let me finish…after the night you came over, I had my mind set. After twenty years of being together, I felt disrespected, devalued, unloved…and that's not something that I'm not willing to put up with, no matter how much I love you. I have never stepped out on you during our relationship. Better yet, I don't think that I've even thought about it. From day one, you have been my everything, and I thought that you felt the same."

As Isabella's words flowed from her lips, all Joe could do was put his head down. He had so much he had to say, that he needed her to know, but as she wished, he remained quiet.

"I was ready to throw in the towel on this whole thing…until I talked to Laura."

"What?" he asked shooting his head up.

"Laura stopped by today, and we got a chance to talk."

"And no blood was shed? The police didn't have to be called?"

"Surprisingly, no," she laughed, "I can admit that at first I had nothing to say to her, and I really felt like she didn't have anything to say to me either, but she wouldn't let up."

"Yeah, that sounds like Laura."

"So I told her that she had five minutes to speak…"

"And?"

"And she made me realize a lot. I know that it was a long time ago, Joe, but I don't think that you were honest with me when we first got together."

"What do you mean?"

"When we met, you told me that you two were separated."

"I…I…"

"It doesn't matter now. I realize that maybe my timing in your life wasn't perfect, but in the grand scheme of things, it was destined. I don't think that you and Laura ever got any closure on your relationship, which is why it was so easy for you to fall back into a situation with her."

"I never meant to let it go that far," he admitted.

"I know, and Laura let me know that too. You should really thank her, you know? She really helped me off a ledge. If she would've never stopped by, your shit would've been on the side of the curb waiting for the garbage man to pick it up."

Joe was shocked that Laura came to speak on his behalf. Through his own confusion, he knew he had hurt her in the process too, but like always, she was looking out for him.

"So what does this mean?" he asked, feeling a little more hopeful.

"If you can say that this thing between you and Laura is really over and that you know exactly where you want to be, I would like to give us another chance."

"Are you serious?" Isabella just smiled. "Laura meant a lot to me growing up. She was my best friend, you know? We both got thrown into this crazy world by our parents, but no matter how crazy it got, I knew that we had each other. Despite all of that, I knew deep down that we just wanted different things out of life. I didn't handle the situation with you or her like a man should have, and I think that's where my guilt came in. After all these years, I realized that Laura didn't deserve to be treated the way I treated her because I was going through something in my own life. I was confused back then. I just wanted to make it right again even if it was after all this time, but I love you, and I know that. You have helped me to become the man I am today. I'm not perfect by any means, and I never will be, but I vow to strive for perfection every single day that I get to wake up next to you. I loved you then, Izzy, and I love you even more now. I am so sorry I hurt you. I just want the chance to make it up to you," he said staring into her eyes.

"Get over here," she said pulling him into her as their lips met.

"I love you," he whispered.

"I know."

$$$$$

After talking to Gabrielle, Jewel was done with the family drama for the day, but he knew he couldn't relax just yet. It was time for him to go home. Despite what he was going through with Reagan, she was still his wife, and she and their family meant everything to him. Not knowing if she was at the house or not, he pulled out his cellphone when another call came through. It was Vanessa.

"Hello?"

"Jewel?" she asked as if she wasn't too sure he'd answer.

"Yeah, it's me. What's up?" he asked as he made his way onto the freeway.

"I need you to meet me somewhere," she hurried to say.

"Listen, Nessa, now is not a really good time for me. I got some shit I need to check up on at the house…and it can't wait. I'll hit you up when I'm done though."

"No, Jewel, you're not understanding me," she said, not able to say too much over the phone, "I'm by the *Carolina's* off Mack. I need you to meet me over here now."

"Nessa, I really…"

"Jewel," she snapped, "I wouldn't be calling you like this if it wasn't important."

"Alright, alright," he said having to place his plans on hold, "Give me like twenty minutes."

As Jewel made his way to the South, he started to get anxious. Vanessa rarely ever called him first unless she had some news for him, and 9 times out of 10, it was never good. Getting off of the freeway to avoid the traffic, he decided to take the back streets. As he mobbed through the lanes, his mind began to race.

What does she need to talk about that's so important? Did they find Dash? A million things began to cross his mind all at once, but he knew he wouldn't get his answers until they met.

Fifteen minutes later, Jewel pulled into the back of the Mexican restaurant he agreed to meet Vanessa at. Not wanting to look suspicious, he slid through the drive-thru.

"Welcome to *Carolina's.* What can I get you?" a woman asked in a deep Spanish-accent.

"Yeah, let me get the carne asada Super Nachos, extra sour cream and guacamole."

"Anything else for you, sir?"

"Yeah, let me get a large horchata too…oh, and some hot sauce."

"Okay, your total comes to $12.64. Pull up to the window."

As Jewel pulled forward, he spotted Vanessa's dark-tinted, black Infinite parked on the other side of the parking lot.

"That'll be $12.64," the woman repeated as Jewel pulled up to the take-out window.

Without looking, he handed her a $20 bill, never taking his eyes off Vanessa. He couldn't see inside, but he hoped she was alone.

"$7.36 is your change," she said before handing him a plastic bag full of greasy Mexican-food and his sweet, milky drink.

"Thank you," he said pulling off.

Parking a couple of stalls down from Vanessa, he sat back until she noticed that he had arrived. Within seconds, she hopped out of her car and made her way over to Jewel's.

Tick. Tick. Tick. Tick. She impatiently tapped on the glass as she waited for him to answer. Unlocking the door, he waited until she was inside before he spoke.

"What's up, Vanessa?"

"Nigga, I know you didn't stop and get nothing to eat," she said looking down at the Styrofoam container filled with chips, grilled meat, and cheese with the works.

"Man, you got my nerves bad. After I roll up, I'm taking these down," he smiled, "You want one?"

"No, thank you. I didn't come to have lunch, Jewel. I needed to talk to you."

"Well, I'm here now. Talk."

"The last time we met up was right after you got shot at, right?"

"Yeah," he said breaking down a swisher, spilling the guts outside the door.

"Well, I told you that I was going to do my best to make it go away…"

"And?" he asked, taking a sip of his horchata.

"And I did."

"So what's the problem?" he asked filling the brown swisher with bright green buds before he licked it and sealed it shut.

"Jewel, you know how I am. When shit doesn't make sense, I let my curiosity get the best of me. I started to look into all the details you gave me…which weren't much I must admit. Anyway…I looked up records for the unmarked Chevy the gunmen were in. Of course, without a license plate number, it was almost impossible to find out any information on it, but I figured that whoever did this had a specific target—you, so it was less likely that they would've used their own car for the hit. I ran some searches through a couple of rental places in Sacramento. One came up with service records for a 2006 black Chevy Impala with license plate number 2ZRX633 the day after the shooting. Whoever was driving that day bapped the car after you returned fire I'm assuming, so there was extreme damage to the front. I looked into it a little further, and I found out that this particular rental car place is on record for renting out cars without the license plates under the table. They rent to people under fake names, no IDs, no credit card information on file, no nothing. For the most part, it looks like they only deal with cash, which make the transactions untraceable."

"Okay…," Jewel said not knowing where Vanessa was going with her story.

"I went down there, and I let the owner of the place know that I could have his whole shit shut down in two seconds if he didn't tell me what I wanted to know."

"Did he cooperate?"

"Is water wet?" she laughed, "Of course, he cooperated. He gave me the full service report, so not only was there damage to the front of the car, but several bullet holes were found in the back and on the right side. I didn't need to involve ballistics to know that those bullets came from your gun. The owner said that he was paid in full for the damage, so there was no reason to raise any red flags."

"Okay, so we have the car, but we still don't know who was in that mothafucka," Jewel sighed, "That honestly doesn't help, Vanessa."

"You didn't let me finish. On the service report, the owner listed the driver as being Cameron A. Michaels, but when I looked this Cameron guy up using the birthdate and driver's license number they had in their system, it wasn't surprising to find out that he doesn't exist."

"I don't understand."

"I went back to the owner, and I let him know that I knew the driver info he had was fraudulent. He admitted that he never got the guy's real name and that the information that he had on file was just for show, but he did say that he was tall, light-skinned with dreads, and had a thick Caribbean accent."

"Caribbean?" he asked, needing her to spell it out for him.

"The guy that shot you, Jewel, is apparently from the islands somewhere."

As soon as the words left her mouth, Jewel felt like time had suddenly stopped.

Fuck! he thought. As much as he didn't want to accept it, there was no denying it anymore. Tusan was their guy.

"So now all I need to do is figure out who this guy is, and…"

"There's no need," Jewel said shaking his head.

"I know that you kinda wanted to leave this one alone, Jewel, but with this guy still out there, we gotta move quickly."

"No…it's not that," he sighed, "I already know who he is."

"What?" she asked turning her body to face him, "Who?"

"Tusan Cole…my new security detail."

"But that doesn't make any sense."

"I know…after I got shot at, my mom brought him in. He's been around ever since, but I never got to meet any of his team until the other day. It makes perfect sense now. He had those niggas moving for him while he just sat back and watched all the shit unfold."

"What happened the other day?" Vanessa questioned. She needed to know everything if she was going to help protect Jewel.

"I went to LA on business. Word was going around that one of Kisino's dudes was behind the hit, so I had him come with me."

"What? Are you fucking stupid?"

"I needed to find out for myself."

"And?"

"And Tusan and his brother hit me with all this fake-ass information about Dash, and I believed them. They had me thinking that he was the one behind the shooting, so I took care of it."

"Jewel, please don't tell me that you…"

"I did what I had to do," he snapped.

"No, you didn't. You should've called me. I could've…"

"He watched Asaya die."

"What?"

"He was there the night Asaya and Pop were killed," he said looking down, "We all thought that it was just Blue and Kisino in the house, but after Blue was shot, Dash climbed out of the window and hid until the scene cleared. I just lost it. I know he didn't pull the trigger, but after hearing that shit, I lost it, and I'm glad I did. Even though he didn't set any of this shit up, he was still a snake, and he got exactly what he deserved. He was gon' have to answer for what he did sooner or later."

"Jewel, I can't help you if you don't let me know what's going on with you. You're creating all this mess for me to clean up, and I don't even know what I'm looking for. Now, we got a body floating around LA somewhere with your name on it."

"Naw, it's good. Even if they find Dash, they won't be able to recognize him."

"What do you mean?"

"Tusan lit his ass up. By the time he got done with him, there was nothing left but ashes. That's why I never suspected him. He was down to ride no matter what, but now I know that was just to keep me close."

"Jewel, this is actually great news!" Vanessa beamed with excitement, "I can have my guys pick him up right now. I know that we can find something to link him back to the shooting. I just need to know where he's at."

"I can't do that, Nessa," he said firing up the blunt he had just rolled.

"Why not?"

"This nigga has violated everything I stand for. I basically served up the M.A.C. Boys to him on a fucking silver platter. You gotta know me by now, Nessa; the last thing I'ma do is snitch on the nigga. I appreciate you and everything you do for me. I mean, you stay looking out for the team, but you do still work for them people. This is some shit I gotta handle on my own."

"Jewel, you sound stupid. This guy has shown you just a glimpse of what he's capable of. Who knows what he's planning next."

"Well, I guess I need to move fast then."

"Let me help you," she pleaded.

"I'll call you if I need you," he said unlocking the doors, "I promise."

Knowing how stubborn Jewel could be, Vanessa decided to leave the situation alone…for now. After Asaya died, she vowed that she would keep his family safe by any means for Chase's sake, and she had no plans on breaking it. Not saying another word, she slipped out of Jewel's car and slowly made her way back to hers as he backed out of the parking lot. He was on a mission.

$$$$$

Ring. Ring. Ring. Ring. "Fuck! I need you to pick up," Jewel said to himself. *Ring. Ring. Ring. Ring. Ring.*

"Hi, you've reached Reagan. Sorry I'm unable to answer your call at this time. Please leave your name and number, and I will call you back at my earliest convenience. Thank you. *Beep.*"

"Rea, it's me. I don't have a lot of time to explain, but I need you to go to my dad's ASAP. I'll explain more later. I have stuff I need to handle, but I promise that as soon as I'm done, I'll be there…I love you," he said hanging up.

Hoping that she was just still mad, Jewel tried to calm his anxiety. He prayed that she was safe. As much as he wanted to run home and hold her in his arms, he knew he couldn't, not yet. If everything about Tusan was true, he knew he had to stay one step ahead. Tusan was out for blood. Jewel just had to figure out why. Trying to make sense of it all, he decided to call Sacario.

"What's up, bruh?" he asked answering on the first ring.

"Listen, nigga, I don't have a lot of time…"

"Yo, what's wrong?" Sacario asked sensing the urgency in his voice.

"I just met up with Vanessa."

"Okay…"

"Long story short, she basically told me the same shit you did earlier about Tusan, but she confirmed that him and his nigga were the ones behind the shooting down at the office."

"Blood, are you serious?"

"I wish I wasn't, but it's no question that he set Smackz and Hassan up. Remember when Sani said that when Tusan got ready to bust back, his gun jammed?"

"Yeah."

"That wasn't by coincidence, bruh. There was no way he was about to take out his own niggas, but he had to look like his life was on the line too."

"Fuck! I can't even believe this shit. I mean, when K came at me about all this, I didn't want to believe that it was really Tusan, feel me? Bruh played the role like a mothafucka."

"Who you telling?"

"So what's the plan?"

"I'm still figuring that out now, so be on standby. I'll call you when I know more, but on mamas, this nigga is gonna die tonight guaranteed."

"Ay, just be careful, blood, and hit me back as soon as you can. You know my trigger finger is itching."

"One."

Finally being able to put the true face to Smackz's killer was bittersweet. He was anxious to avenge his cousin, but he was mad at himself for letting Tusan and his team get so close. Needing to get his mind right, Jewel found himself in front of Khailiah's place. If no one else could, he knew that she would be able to talk some sense back into him. With everything going on, his mind was racing, and he couldn't afford to make any more mistakes.

Looking down at his phone sitting in the middle console, he realized that Reagan still hadn't called him back.

She can't be that mad, he thought to himself, *Maybe she didn't get the message yet.*

Rea, I know that you're probably still mad at me, he texted her, *and honestly, you have every right to be. I fucked up. I know that, but I need you to put that aside for right now. Take Chase to my dad's and wait for me there. I promise I won't be long. I love you.*

After pressing *Send*, Jewel hopped out of his car and made his way towards Khailiah's front door.

Ding. Dong.

"Hey, J," she said quickly opening the door once she saw his car parked outside in the driveway.

"Hey," he said walking inside, not having time for the pleasantries.

"I wished you would've called me earlier to let me know that you were still coming. I would've cooked us dinner or something. I got some leftover catfish in the fridge if you're hungry."

"Naw, I'm good right now," he said pulling out the blunt he had put out earlier and tucked behind his ear. Without even asking for permission, he fired up again, hoping to calm his nerves as he leaned back against the couch.

"You cool?" Khailiah laughed, "You seem a little stressed out."

"Sit down," he instructed.

"Jewel, what is it?" she asked fidgeting a little as she played with the heart pendent that sat against her chest, "You're scaring me."

"You know Tusan, my security, right?" She remained silent. "Did he ever come down to the office while I wasn't there, or has he ever shown up here?"

"Why you asking me that?"

"I just got word that him and his niggas were the ones behind the shooting down at the office, and they were the ones who killed Smackz." Khailiah put her head down. "I obviously didn't catch the shit, but did he ever do anything weird? I'm just tryna figure out where the nigga got his information from. It's like he knew everything about the M.A.C. Boys, shit only a mothafucka on the inside should've known."

"Jewel, that's what I've been meaning to talk to you about," Khailiah said standing up.

"Talk to me about what?"

"So you know that Golden was the one who originally hired me, but because of some other-ass shit, he had me go to Barbados to help out your mom and your uncle."

"Yeah, I know that," he said taking a drag from the swisher that sat against his lips.

"Well, because everyone believed that Golden only hired me so he could fuck me, no one really took me seriously. I never got the respect I felt like I deserved as a professional, so I basically became like an errand girl. While I was in Barbados, I had a lot of free-time on my hands. I used to travel through the island 'cause I was bored and lonely, and that's when I met…Tusan."

"What?" Jewel asked as he shot up, "You know this nigga?"

"We dated for a few years until I moved back to Sacramento to work for you. We broke up because I didn't want to do the long-distance thing, but after he found out who you really were, he came out here too."

"What are you talking about?"

"…for the past year, I've been giving him information about the M.A.C. Boys. It was me."

"What?" Jewel yelled as he rushed over to her and wrapped his hand around her neck, pushing her against the wall.

"That…was before I…got to know you," she struggled to say, "When I started to…have feelings…for you, I told him that I couldn't…anymore."

"Then how did my cousin end up dead?" he snapped.

"Tusan told me that if I didn't continue to cooperate, he was gonna kill me," she cried, "I was scared. I know that it's no excuse, but you don't know Tusan like I do. I knew he meant that shit."

"So all along it's been you?" Jewel asked in disbelief as he paced back and forth in the living room, "All this fucking time, it was you? You made a nigga think you had feelings for me just so you could set me up? Bitch, I promise you didn't have to do all that."

"I swear I wanted to tell you. You have no idea how many times I wanted to tell you."

"Is that supposed to make shit better? I trusted you. You had me ready to give up on my marriage all for you to be playing me?"

"No, Jewel," she pleaded, "My feelings for you are real. I love you, and I know that you love me too." She tried to reach for his hand, but he quickly snatched away from her. "Please don't do this," she said as tears rolled down her face, "I can fix this. I can fix this…I swear I never thought that it would go this far. He said that after he got the money he needed, he was going back home. He promised me that no one was gonna get hurt."

"Money?" Jewel laughed, "Bitch, I could've gave you some money."

"I gave all the money back."

"What?"

"The money I got from Tusan…I gave it all back. I didn't want it. $100,000 isn't worth losing you."

"$100,000? You mean that money you had up in this mothafucka was from the warehouse they hit up?" he yelled, snatching her up by her hair.

"Owwwwww," she screamed as his grip got tighter.

"What does he want?" Jewel asked through his teeth.

"I don't know…I swear," Khailiah said grabbing ahold of his hand but to no relief.

"Well, I guess we're both about to find out."

"How?" she winced in pain.

"Call him!"

Chapter Sixteen

"Thank you so much for today," Reagan smiled, "It's been a minute since I've been out to eat."

"Yuh are mo' den welcome, Reagan," Tusan said as they walked inside the house.

After picking up Chase from daycare, the last place she wanted to be was at home alone without Jewel…again. She knew Tusan had work to do, but she had to admit that she was enjoying his company more than she expected.

"If you have to go, I completely understand. I know I've been a little selfish with your time today."

"Yuh kickin' mi out?" he laughed.

"Of course not…you can stay as long as you want."

"Mi would like dah."

"Okay, well, let me just go lay Chase down, and I'll be right back," she said walking up the stairs.

What am I doing? Reagan thought, *If Jewel knew this nigga was here by himself, he would flip out…well, good!*

As much as she missed Jewel, she would be lying if she said that she wasn't hurt. She loved him and desperately wanted their marriage to work, but she was tired of wanting it for the both of them. Something had to give.

After laying Chase down in his bed, she turned off the light and turned on the baby monitor that she had downstairs.

"If he can do this shit, then I can too," she said to herself, freshening up her face in the bathroom mirror before making her way back to Tusan. "Tusan?" she called out once she walked down the stairs.

"Mi in here," he replied from the kitchen.

When Reagan walked in, two glasses of red Chateau Margaux sat on the countertop next to him.

"Mi hope yuh don' mind. Yuh seem stress, so mi thought yuh could use someting ta relax."

"It's like you read my mind," she laughed as she pulled out a barstool and sat down.

"Still no word from Jewel?" Tusan questioned.

"I think he called a little earlier, but I'm not thinking about his ass. If he wants to talk to me, he can come the fuck home," she said rolling her eyes, "But let's not talk about him."

"Wuh yuh wan' ta talk 'bout den?" he asked moving in closer as Reagan became intoxicated by the smell of his cologne mixed with the scent of weed smoke.

"Anything but Jewel," she said looking up into his dark-brown eyes.

Tusan slowly bent down as his dreads caressed the sides of her face attempting to do what he had been longing to do all day. Feeling his lips almost touch hers, Reagan jumped back, knocking the red wine out of his hand and all over his crisp white shirt.

"Oh, my god," she said covering her mouth, "I am so sorry. It's just that when you…I just thought…I'm not…"

"It's good," Tusan laughed, "It's jes a shirt. Mi can get a new one. Don' worry."

Soaking wet from the red liquid that continued to spread, he slipped off his shirt exposing his rock hard, caramel-colored body, he watched Reagan's expression change. She couldn't keep her eyes off him.

"…le-let me get you another shirt," she offered.

"Naw, dah's okay. Mi jes wait fuh dis one ta dry," he said dabbing the wine off of his chest and abs with a paper towel.

"That's silly. Then you'd just be walking around with a big-ass stain on your shirt, and I know you're too fly for that. I'm pretty sure Jewel has something that you can fit."

"Mi good, Reagan. Mi promise…unless, dis is mekin' yuh uncomfortable," he said staring at her.

"No, no…I'm fine," she swallowed. As she traced his muscles with her eyes, it didn't take long before she noticed the black and purple bruised dent that sat on the left side of his chest.

"What happened?" she asked as she reached up to touch the healing wound.

"Long story…," he said grabbing her hand before she could.

"I'm no expert, but from the looks of it, it looks like a bullet wound."

"Someting like dah," Tusan said not wanting to go into detail.

"So you're not gonna tell me what happened?" she laughed.

"To be honest, mi was shot a while-back, but mi had a vest pun, so…"

Suddenly, Tusan's phone began to ring, and he thanked the universe for the distraction. When he looked down at the screen, he knew he had to answer.

"Reagan, mi tink dah mi will tek dah shirt afta-all."

"Okay," she said unable to take her eyes off his chest. He may have not wanted to talk about it, but she knew a bullet wound when she saw one. "I'ma get you some gauze and alcohol wipes too. I don't think it's good to have that shit just out in the open like that."

"Thank you," he smiled.

"I'll be right back."

He waited for her to leave the kitchen before he answered the phone.

"Wuh is it, bae?"

"We have a problem."

"Not now, Khailiah. Mi gon' have ta call yuh back," Tusan whispered as he made his way across the kitchen, "Mi workin' right now."

"Jewel knows everything," she blurted out.

"Wuh?!"

"I was down at the office today, and he cornered me. He said that he knows that you were the one behind all this and that I helped."

"Dah's impossible."

"Well, it's true. What do you want me to do?"

"Weh are yuh?"

"I left before things got any crazier. Jewel trashed the office. I was scared of what he was gonna do next. I'm in my car in the parking lot across the street."

"Don' worry, K. Mi pun mi way. Jes stay dere, okay?"

"What other choice do I have?"

"Dis shit's been goin' pun fuh too long. Jewel's been pun borrowed time. Now, it's time ta end dis shit once and fuh all."

As Reagan made her way back to the kitchen with a fresh shirt in hand, she overheard Jewel's name, so she fell back, being nosey.

"He knows you had Smackz set up to be murdered. Tusan, if he catches me, I know I'm next," she cried.

"Khailiah, mi have everyting unda control. Mi jes need yuh ta stay put. Jewel is not stupid. He won' touch you. His beef is wit' me, an' mi plan to mek him suffa fuh all dah his family has done ta mine."

"What about Reagan?"

"Dis bitch is a waste of mi time. Mi thought dah mi would be able ta get some infamation from her, but all she wan' ta do is complain 'bout dis nigga."

"Are you gonna kill her too?" Khailiah asked as her voice started to shake.

"Of course," he laughed, "But mi rather tek care of dis first. Wifey can wait. Stay in yuh car. Mi pun de way now. Mi should be at the office in twenty." Tusan hung up the phone, and when he spun around, Reagan was standing right in front of him.

"I got the shirt," she smiled.

"Yuh scare de hell out of mi, gyal," he said grabbing his chest.

"Everything okay? You seem tense."

"Yeah, someting came up. Mi would love ta stay here wit' yuh, but yuh know…business ain't gon' deal wit' itself."

"You sure you have to go now? I mean, this bottle isn't gonna finish itself," she laughed.

"Mi be back…mi promise," he said as he made his way out of the front door.

$$$$$

Jewel and Khailiah sat inside her car waiting for Tusan to arrive.

"I texted him that I was at the top," she said looking over at Jewel, "What are gonna do to him?"

"What I should've done a long time ago," he admitted as he caressed the gun that sat in his lap.

"I'm sorry, Jewel. I know that my word doesn't mean shit to you right now, but I need you to know that my feelings for you are real. I love you…"

"Khailiah, please just shut up."

"I love you more than I've ever loved Tusan. All of this was a mistake. I know I should've told you about what he was up to sooner…especially before anyone got hurt, but I was scared for my own life. When Tusan feels like he's been crossed, there's nothing that can stop him from getting revenge…"

"Shut up," Jewel yelled, "I don't give a fuck about whatever you're talking about. You're lucky that I don't put a bullet in your head myself."

"But, Jewel..."

"You made your choice, so fucking deal with it," he said not even bothering to look her way, "After this shit is over, you can kick rocks. I never want to see you again."

Suddenly, they both heard a car racing through the darkened garage.

"Let's go," Jewel said pointing his gun at her as she slowly made her way out of the car. Walking over to the passenger's side, he snatched her by her arm and put his finger up to lips. "Shhhhhhhhhh," he said as they disappeared into the shadows.

Spotting Khailiah's car, Tusan rushed to park beside her.

"K, K...," he shouted as he got out.

Wasting no time, Jewel pushed her from around the wall they were hiding behind and said, "You looking for her, bruh?"

All Tusan could do was laugh. "Mi knew it," he said shaking his head.

"So this is who you had on the inside, blood? I must admit ya'll both had everybody fooled."

"Dah was de point, Jewel, but mi knew dah soona or lata, she was gon' mek her loyalties clear, an' *poof,* here yuh are."

"This bitch doesn't give a fuck about nobody but herself," he said snatching off the necklace he had given her from around her neck before pushing her into Tusan, "She's your problem now."

"Jewel," Khailiah said as tears began to roll down her cheeks.

"Yuh really cryin', Kahialih? Ova dis nigga?" Tusan barked.

"I love him," she whispered.

"Like mi said befo', mi was already aware dah she turn pun mi. Mi honestly have no mo' use fuh her." In one swift motion, Tusan pulled out his gun, placed the barrel against the side of her head, and quickly pulled the trigger. *POP!* He watched in amusement as her body dropped to the concrete. "Yuh really should have done betta, Jewel. Khailiah is not a good actress. Mi knew dah she was up ta someting. Mi jes no expec' her ta be dis stupid."

Jewel couldn't take his eyes off of her lifeless face as Tusan continued to speak.

"Don' feel bad fuh her, Jewel. She knew all along wuh de plan was, an' she had no problem helpin' mi every step of de way."

"Why me?" He needed to know.

"Why yuh?" Tusan laughed, "Yuh can't be serious."

"Nigga, I don't have time for all this. You better tell me something before I blow your fucking brains out," Jewel said raising his gun to his face.

"Yuh family owes mi," Tusan said before he punched Jewel in the mouth, making him drop his gun. Grabbing Jewel by his shirt, he continued to punch him in his ribs, knocking the air out of him with every blow. "Mi whole reason fuh bein' here is ta mek yuh an' yuh family suffa," he said through his teeth.

Trying to catch his breath, Jewel struggled to stand to his feet. Tusan only gave him a moment's relief before he punched him in the jaw. Jewel felt the blood spill from his mouth as his lip split.

"Yuh really don' know, do yuh?" he asked as he dragged Jewel over to the edge of the garage. Jewel turned his head and felt sick seeing how high up they actually were. "Dah meks dis even betta."

"What do you…want?" Jewel finally managed to say.

"Yuh blood…," Tusan said hanging his body over the ledge, "Yuh uncle kill mi fatha, an' now mi gonna mek sure dah he loses everyone 'round him too."

"What?"

"Stevin had mi fatha murder. He tinks dah no one knows, but mi know dah it was him. Ever since mi had ta put mi fatha in de ground, mi made it mi mission ta put de ones he love in de ground too. It was jes luck dah de first person we hit was his own son, an' now yuh next. Rememba, blood is *always* thicka den wata."

Tusan's grip around Jewel's throat got tighter, and Jewel became light-headed as his body continued to drop further and further down the side. Just as Tusan was about to let him go, he heard the door that led to the stairwell slam shut. When he looked up, he saw Reagan standing there.

"Where's Jewel?" she demanded to know.

"'Bout ta meet his maka," Tusan laughed, "But mi glad yuh came ta enjoy de show, baby."

"Let him go," she said rushing over towards the ledge when she tripped over Khailiah's dead body, "Oh, my god!"

As much as Reagan hated her, she never would have wanted to see her end up like that.

"Let him go!" she repeated, pulling a gun from behind her back. With her hands shaking, she slowly aimed it at his head.

"Mi no tink yuh wan' ta do dah, mamas," Tusan smiled as he dropped Jewel a little lower, taunting her.

BOW!

Reagan let off a shot hitting Tusan in the shoulder. Wincing in pain, he let Jewel go.

"Ahhhhhhhhhhhhhhhhhhh!"

"Jewel," Reagan screamed.

Tusan struggled to reach for his gun, but before he could, she let off another shot, this time, hitting him in the chest. *BOW!* Tusan dropped to his knees as blood spilled from his mouth before he slumped over.

"Jewel?" Reagan yelled again.

Not prepared for what she was about to see, she walked slowly over to the railing he had just fell from with tears in her eyes, but when she looked down, she saw him hanging on to the side of the latticed metal siding as his feet dangled.

"Oh, my gosh, Jewel," she screamed out in relief as her heart continued to beat out of her chest.

"Reagan, I need you to help pull me up."

"Hold on, baby," she said placing the gun back in the waistband of her jeans. She bent over the railing and extended her arms as far as she could until he grabbed her hands. Struggling to pull him up, she held on with all of her might as Jewel reached up for the railing. Finally getting a grip, he hoisted himself back over and fell down to the concrete. As he laid on his back and looked up into the night's sky, he didn't know what to say.

"Jewel, are you okay?" Reagan asked, rushing to be by his side.

"Rea, how did you...when did you?" he asked, struggling to catch his breath.

"Shhhhhhh," she said putting her finger to his lips, "Tusan was at the house earlier when he got a phone call. I heard him say your name, but the more I listened, I realized that he was trying to set you up and that Khailiah was in on it too. He said he was coming down here to the office, so I knew I had to follow him. After he left, that's when I got your messages. I hurried to drop Chase off with Joe and Isabella, and after that, I came straight here. I had no idea, Jewel."

"Reagan, I'm sorry...I didn't mean to put you through this," he said struggling to sit up.

"We have to do something, J," she said beginning to panic, "Khailiah's dead...what do we do?"

"Jewel?" they both heard someone say from within the darkness.

When he looked up, he saw Vanessa running towards them.

"Vanessa? What are you doing here?" he asked rubbing the side of his face, trying to stop the blood that continued to flow.

"I followed you here."

"How?"

"I kinda put a tracker on your phone," she admitted.

"What?"

"You left me no choice, Jewel. I knew you needed my help, but as usual, you're too stubborn to ask for it. I'm glad I did though. What happened?" she asked looking at all of the blood that covered the ground.

"I told you I'd handle it," he said finally standing to his feet.

"Jewel, you have two dead bodies up here. I'ma need more than that."

"Kha…Khailiah was the informant. She had been feeding Tusan information about the M.A.C. Boys for the past year."

"So you killed her?" Vanessa asked, needing him to say anything other than yes.

"No," he said putting his head down. As much as it hurt him to know that she had betrayed him, he couldn't deny that his feelings for her were real. He wished things would've worked out differently, but he knew that paying for her sins was inevitable.

"Once Tusan found out that Khailiah told me everything, he killed her."

"And Tusan?"

"Vanessa, I'm pretty sure you can figure out what happened next."

"Jewel, now is not the time…give me your gun."

"What?"

"If I'm going to fix this, I'ma need your gun," she said holding out her hand.

After looking over at Jewel, Reagan slowly slipped the gun from behind her back and handed it to Vanessa.

"How the fuck do you expect me to help you when you insist on lying to me about every-fucking-thing, Jewel?" she yelled.

"You can't expect me to implicate my wife."

"Her fucking fingerprints are all over this thing," Vanessa snatching the gun from Reagan's hand, "Go!"

"What?"

"Let me do my job, Jewel. Go!"

Without saying another word, he grabbed Reagan's hand as they walked back towards the stairwell. Before they descended down the stairs, Jewel bent down and picked up his gun, slipping it in his back pocket before Vanessa could notice.

"Jewel, is this shit finally over?" Reagan asked as she looked up at him.

"For now," he said as they disappeared into the shadows.

The End

Available on Amazon, Barnes & Noble, and Google Play!

All Tamara Wright had in this world was her family...that was until she met Snake. Tired of her mother's rigid rules, she grew hungry for her freedom when she finally noticed the world that was all around her. Throwing caution to the wind, Tamara runs right into the arms of her awaiting lover and soon finds out that everything that glitters with Snake is not gold once he's taken away from her for good.

Caught up in the flashing lights and fast life, Tamara finds herself falling in love...with only the money, and through Snake's guidance, "Bossy Monroe" is born. At 17, Tamara found herself alone with nowhere to go and with skills that only translated to the streets, but refusing to admit defeat and go back home to her mom and little brother, she decides to get it how she lives with her best friend Chinx when they decide to put together the ultimate money move, but in the end, no one wins.

With Love, Lies, Murder, and Betrayal, Tamara will have to choose once of for all if anything means more to her than the Almighty Dollar.

From schemes to a diva sitting pretty, see how it all began.

www.blackedenpublications.com

Available on Amazon! FREE with *Kindle Unlimited*

Tony Jones was bred into a life that he could not control. He vowed to walk in the steps of his father to keep his family accustomed to the life they used to have, but no matter how hard he tried, he would never be Anthony Jones, Sr. After serving over ten years in prison, Anthony planned to rebuild his empire with his two sons by his side, but Tony had other plans. With the opportunity of a lifetime in clear view, Tony finally found his path in life outside of Anthony's shadows, but he wasn't so sure that his father was willing to let go.

www.blackedenpublications.com

Available on Amazon! FREE with *Kindle Unlimited*

Due to a broken heart, Trina Mitchell became an opportunist in every sense of the word. It was always "Fuck niggas, get money", but when she meets Jonah Lee, leader of the Rich Gang, she falls head over heels in love with his fat pockets and endless influence. Jonah was a pillar for all those around him, but he poisoned the same community he tried so desperately to save, and Trina never saw his vision until it was too late. After a tragic loss for the Rich Gang, she unsuspectingly replaces Jonah as leader hoping that his legacy would live on through her, but she soon finds out that love, lost, betrayal, and murder are all aligned in her path. Is she strong enough to wear the crown?

www.blackedenpublications.com

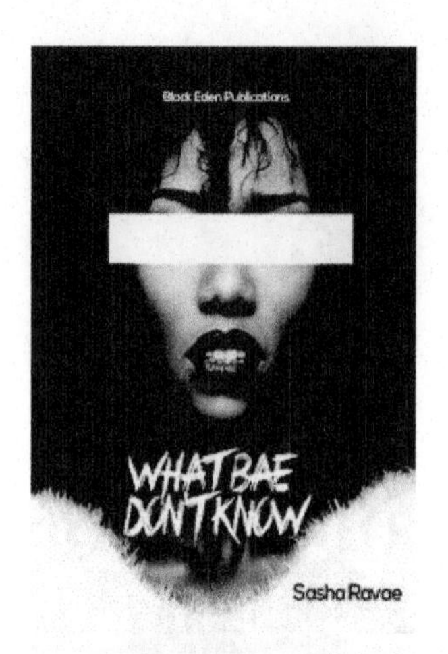
Black Eden Publications
WHAT BAE
DON'T KNOW
Sasha Ravae

BLACK EDEN PUBLICATIONS PRESENTS
CITY
NIGHTS
SASHA RAVAE
&SEQUAIA

Black Eden Publications

Please send order form to:

Black Eden Publications, LLC

P.O. Box 3375, Hayward, CA 94540

info@blackedenpublications.com

www.blackedenpublications.com

Thank you for your order!

Shipping Information:

Date: ____________

Name: ____________________________

Address: ___________________________

Email: ____________________ (Optional)

City/State/Zip: ________________ ______ __________

Pricing:

a. Shipping + $3.00
b. Receive a 15% discount when you order **5 or more books** during the same order.

Title	Price	# of Books	Total
Boy Toy	**$15**		**$**
City Nights	**$15**		**$**
Cocoa Baby	**$15**		**$**
Counterfeit Dreams	**$15**		**$**
Counterfeit Dreams 2: A Hustler's Hope	**$15**		**$**
Counterfeit Dreams 3: A Dream's Nightmare	**$15**		**$**
Counterfeit Dreams 4: A Dream's Nightmare	**$15**		**$**
Counterfeit Dreams 5: When Dreams Aren't Enough	**$15**		**$**
Counterfeit Dreams: The Complete Collection	**$50**		**$**
Disciple in America: A Teenage Guide to Faith	**$10**		**$**
Dying for Change	**$15**		**$**
Love, Lies, and Vendettas	**$15**		**$**
Love, Lies, and Vendettas 2	**$15**		**$**
Love, Lies, and Vendettas 3	**$15**		**$**

"Welcome to the Inner Circle..."

Ski Mask Divas	**$15**		**$**
Ski Mask Schemes	**$15**		**$**
Trap Goddess	**$15**		**$**
What Bae Don't Know	**$15**		**$**

Payment (Check appropriate box):

- ☐ Money Order
- ☐ Check
- ☐ Pay Using Credit Card (Please contact info@blackedenpublications.com for invoice)

"Welcome to the Inner Circle..."

CPSIA information can be obtained
at www.ICGtesting.com
Printed in the USA
LVOW04s1758101016
508154LV00015B/1290/P